PEDRA CANGA

Tereza Albues

PEDRA CANGA

*Translated from the Portuguese
by Clifford E. Landers*

●

MASTERWORKS OF FICTION

(1987)

GREEN INTEGER
KØBENHAVN & LOS ANGELES
2001

GREEN INTEGER
Edited by Per Bregne
København/Los Angeles

Distributed in the United States by Consortium Book
Sales and Distribution, 1045 Westgate Drive, Suite 90
Saint Paul, Minnesota 55114-1065

(323) 857-1115 / http://www.greeninteger.com

10 9 8 7 6 5 4 3 2 1

Design: Per Bregne
Typography: Guy Bennett
Photograph: Photograph of Tereza Albues
by Fernando Natalici

LIBRARY OF CONGRESS CATALOGING IN PUBLICATION DATA
Albues, Tereza
Pedra Canga
ISBN: 1-892295-70-9
p. cm — Green Integer 32
I. Title II. Series III. Translation

Printed in the United States of America on acid-free paper.

To my husband Rob with love

If you don't have the courage to jump the back-yard fence, how will you manage the gate to the world?

—ZÉ GARBAS

It takes a long time for the eyes to see clearly and free themselves of preconceptions.

—MARCOLA

On the night Mr. V. lay dying, a storm unlike any ever seen in these parts flattened trees, houses, chicken coops, pigsties, and lampposts. The howling wind was so strong that the frightened domestic animals tried to take refuge inside the house, while others fled in terror for parts unknown. There was even the case of the mason Augusto Campo Belo's pet goat, which was never found.

"The goat got caught up in a ferocious whirlwind and the Evil One hauled it off into the earth," said Rita Maria, Campo Belo's wife.

A lightning bolt struck the small power plant, leaving Pedra Canga in total darkness. The people, frightened half to death, clutched their saints. You could see people kneeling before their prayer alcoves, intoning litanies, asking St. Barbara to calm the tempest, making vows–some impossible of fulfillment–in exchange for an answer to their prayers.

Maria Belarmina, some 17 years later, would disagree with the beginning of this account. "It wasn't nighttime at all. Everything happened around three in the afternoon. The whole world got dark all of a sudden and we had to light lamps for a time, because in those days there weren't any electric lights, no ma'm. The storm was fierce and it wasn't the kind sent by God. Something evil was commanding the winds. I've heard the wind howl many a time, but never like that. It sounded like the howling of a mad dog or a starving wolf. And there was the sound of drums, laughter, crying, screaming, cursing, all mixed together with a stench so unbearable that we had to keep our noses covered."

"It was the kingdom of the Unspeakable taking over the earth," said Ludovica, obviously to avoid mentioning the name of the One with Horns.

Neco Silvino, Maria Belarmina's husband, swore he'd seen a headless mule, braying and spitting fire in a crazed dash, break through the estate fence and plunge headlong into the underbrush toward the Vergare house. Many had blind faith in Neco Silvino, an old fisherman and teller of ghostly tales, a man on intimate terms with things from beyond.

"I don't run away 'less I know what I'm running from," he always said.

But my grandfather Zé Garbas, who sang and played the guitar and was known in those parts as "Old Sulfurmouth," spoke up, ready to put the lie to the fisherman.

"Don't you believe a word of it. I've known him since childhood. He's a born liar."

And to back up what he said, he picked up the guitar. The verse came easily:

> Neco Silvino, a fisherman,
> Who catches only wind
> I've known you since we both were boys
> Your lies you must defend
> But even cornered by a cutlass
> I'd swear to heaven that you're gutless.

But those who sided with Neco Silvino still remembered the terrible story he had told, less than three days after it happened. And here's the story just as he spelled it out in detail, after the third round of rum at the Gimme More bar, whose owner Mané Pitchpenny is still alive to call me on it if I'm lying.

"I was on my way back from fishing late one night when I heard a woman's screams coming from the direction of the Mangueiral estate. I brought the canoe up to the edge of the bank, pricked up my ears and squinted. That was when I saw in the distance a huge fire and people dancing around it. Right in the middle was a woman tied to a tree, howling like a mad dog and begging, 'For the love of God, don't put out my eye!' Then I heard an angry, hoarse voice shouting, 'Don't speak that name, you wretched woman. This is the kingdom of Satan. And it is for love of him that we are going to sacrifice your eye.' I didn't hear the rest. I tried to get out of there as fast as I could. It was a dark night, no stars, lots of wind, and I was a long way off, but even so I can swear it was a horrible scene. It really was! Even today my hair stands on end when I remember the poor woman's screams."

The customers in the bar, their eyes glued on Neco Silvino, listened in horror to the fisherman's experience. Suddenly, Big Tomás, a mulatto who stood almost six and a half feet tall, son of the farmer Inocêncio Martins, whose lands bordered the Mangueiral farm, got up and said that was nothing; something a lot worse had happened to his father. Everyone turned to him and said in unison, "Tell us about it, tell us." Big Tomás squatted on the floor and, in a low voice as if recounting a secret of state, began:

"Well, first off I got to say that the Vergare family really does have a pact with Old Nick. There's no other way to explain what happened to my father. It was like this: He woke up one night hearing a funny sound coming from the fence on the Mangueiral side. He got up, grabbed his shotgun, and headed over there. From a distance he saw a dark shape he couldn't rightly make out. He cocked the gun, got closer, and saw an enormous peccary nosing around the fence, trying to knock down the main fence post. My father didn't think twice. He fired straight into the animal's heart. Nothing happened. The animal stood up on its hind legs, looked at my father with fire coming out of its eyes, bared its teeth, and gave out a laugh that shook the woods for miles around. That was when my father saw the animal had a man's face, and guess whose face it was? Colonel Totonho, the spitting image. My father stood there paralyzed, so scared he couldn't run. He started praying, asking for protection from his guardian angel and Our Lady of Guidance. Then he was lucky enough to remember to get a couple of twigs and make a cross and point it toward the monster. When it saw the cross, it started to howl and lit out for the river, disappearing into the darkness. My father, more dead than alive, went home but couldn't fall asleep. He strung his hammock on the porch, rolled a straw cigarette, and stayed there in a stupor, thinking, till daybreak."

I remember that at the end of the story everyone was frightened and since it was already past ten o'clock, each one sought to hit the road for home and safety.

"That's right, you don't mess around with things from the other world," Big Tomás concluded.

THE MANGUEIRAL ESTATE had belonged to the Vergares since nobody could rightly say when. Bento Sagrado, who was the oldest person in Pedra Canga and had lived there longer than anyone, used to tell a story of death and treachery through which they were said to have taken possession of the property. According to him, the true owner of the lands had been Antônio dos Anjos, killed in an ambush at the Vergares' orders, and soon after the crime his widow, Maria dos Anjos, was forced by Colonel Totonho to sign a deed in favor of the powerful Vergare family.

"The poor woman was driven off her land at the end of a whip, in total humiliation. She lived out her days in hiding like a criminal, in fear of the Vergares, who had sworn to kill her if she dared set foot anywhere near Pedra Canga. I never saw such injustice in my life."

My grandfather Zé Garbas disagreed entirely with Bento Sagrado.

"The story's completely different. Maria dos Anjos was the one who ordered the crime, everybody knows that. Why try to hide the truth?"

To the sound of his guitar, he sang to the four winds the story that he supposed to be the only true one about Maria dos Anjos.

"This story was told me by my grandfather Don Garanhon y Garbas Gutierrez, an honored member of the Third Order of St. Joaquim Lampejante of the Incandescent Pamplonas."

No one knew what Order that was, but many were impressed by the pomp of the name. At baptisms and weddings they would ask my grandfather to sing the song about Maria dos Anjos. Sometimes he categorically refused, but when he was in "good spirits" he would puff out his chest and put his voice to work:

> No angel that Maria
> Paint her beauty I cannot
> Woman so infernal
> Went and had her husband shot
> Hitched up with the Colonel
> A man every gal was after
> But no sooner did they marry
> And then justice did not tarry
> They found her body bobbing
> In the river Saranzal
> And so Colonel Totonho
> Came to own the Mangueiral

The fame of Maria dos Anjos's beauty spread far and wide. Some said it got as far as Corumbá, and this despite the only form of transportation being the Guaporé boat, which took over two months to arrive at the border city.

"She was a beautiful and immaculate woman who loved her husband above all else. She was a victim of fate," Maria Belarmina declared emphatically.

"I think so too," Felícia said in support. "Why is it the woman always gets blamed for everything?"

Felícia was firmly convinced that the whole thing was nothing but one slander on top of another. Dona Virgulina, her mother, had been a servant of Maria dos Anjos for many years and said that her mistress was an angel of goodness, a very giving person with a kind heart who suffered at the suffering of others.

Maria dos Anjos was a devout follower of St. Rita of Cássia and had a prayer niche in her bedroom with the saint's image and Guardian Angels on each side. There she said her prayers every night before going to sleep.

"I don't ask only for myself. I ask for all those who live in this vale of tears," she would tell Dona Virgulina.

"A true saint," said Ludovica, for whom the sole culprit of everything was Colonel Totonho, "that spawn of the Hound."

When Maria Belarmina asked Felícia what she thought of my grandfather's songs about Maria dos Anjos, she quickly replied that no one would pay any attention to a "talkative old fool" like him instead of listening to the crystaline truth spoken by a man of integrity like Bento Sagrado, who knew the facts down to the last detail.

Cesário Celestino, an old friend of my father's, said that he'd heard from his grandfather, Colonel Nicomedes, a story that didn't jibe with any of the others.

"Grandpa Nicomedes was a serious and respected man, famous for not mincing words."

He told me that, according to his grandfather, Antônio dos Anjos was a cruel and bloody man with over 30 deaths to his account. A hired killer. If anybody wanted to get rid of somebody else, all they had to do was contract for his services, pay a large amount, and set the date of the crime. The intended victim could commend his soul to the Creator, because the shot wouldn't miss.

"You can count on your fingers the ones who survived ambushes set up by Antônio dos Anjos, and one of them was Colonel Totonho."

"Colonel Totonho? Are you sure?" I asked incredulously.

"Yes m'am, I remember very well hearing that name from my grandfather's lips."

"But who hired Antônio dos Anjos to kill Colonel Totonho?"

"Mr. Tibúrcio Genovez, the powerful mill owner and political leader of Aricá-Mirim. But it backfired," he continued. "Teodoro Janjão, Colonel Totonho's hired gun, was quicker, and Antônio dos Anjos was found the next morning by the bank of the Saranzal. Him and his wife, Maria dos Anjos."

"Why her? They say she was a saint."

"Vermin is more like it. She helped her husband in the killings. Since she was very pretty, she used her beauty to lure the victims."

"But I heard that Antônio dos Anjos was the legitimate owner of the Mangueiral."

"That's just something people made up. What happened was that Mr. Tibúrcio promised to give him the lands for the murder of Colonel Totonho but Antônio dos Anjos died before he ever crossed the Mangueiral boundary line."

My father became angry when I told him of the conversation I'd had with Cesário Celestino. He said he didn't have the faintest idea where his friend had gotten that story from; it must be hardening of the arteries or something worse if he didn't respect even the memory of Colonel Nicomedes....

"What leaves me flabbergasted is how he made up such a complicated intrigue, turning the facts upside

down, slandering the good people and making inno-
cents out of the real culprits. He must be crazy. I'm
going to have a talk with that scatterbrain this very
day."

"Then you think Antônio dos Anjos and his wife
were people of integrity?"

"Of course! People of integrity, held in high esteem
by rich and poor alike. The rightful owners of the
Mangueiral. They came from an illustrious and highly
regarded family from the area. That's what I always
heard from the old folks, while the Vergares were crimi-
nals, perverse, hated by lots of people."

My mother, on the other hand, when consulted on
the subject, said she knew nothing about the matter.

"As long as I've been aware, those folks there, the
Vergares, have owned the Mangueiral. It's best to leave
everything the way it is. I have nothing to gain by
dredging up the past."

On one point everyone was in agreement: Mr.
Verônico Vergare became the rightful owner of the
Mangueiral once he inherited the property from his
father, Colonel Totonho Vergare.

WHAT WENT ON at the Mangueiral was a mystery to the residents of Pedra Canga. The estate was surrounded by high walls topped with broken glass and, at some places, thick barbed wire reinforced what needed no reinforcement. The rear faced the Saranzal river, which served both as a natural boundary line and as protection, for that part of the river was full of whirlpools and undercurrents. River serpents had been seen there, and the banks were always teeming with alligators. It was said that the Vergares fed the beasts on purpose so they would remain there as guards, driving away the curious. But who would dare fish or swim in that area? Even the upriver boatmen with their reputation for bravery passed through there at full speed.

"Lean on the oars and have faith in St. Peter," they said in one voice.

After what happened with Miro Curimbatá, the thing was not to push your luck. Neco Silvino told me that a pack of alligators had swamped the canoe carrying Curimbatá and another friend, Chico Nepomuceno.

"The two of them tried to swim but Curimbatá hadn't gone three strokes when a river serpent swallowed him up. Nepomuceno escaped and is there as witness for anybody that cares to listen. Sure, lots of people don't believe him 'cause the poor guy's 'soft in the head.' But who wouldn't be after something like that?"

In the middle of the estate stood an enormous two-story house in colonial style, of undefined color, a mixture of brown and green, with immense doorways of canga stone, windows and doors of rosewood, with wrought-iron hinges. It was permanently sealed and silent. Fierce dogs guarded the entrance and never left it. They either had feet of lead or had been very well trained not to abandon their post on pain of losing their daily ration of bloody meat.

The estate had plants of every kind: oranges, bananas, manioc, squash, potatoes, cashews, mangoes, pitombas, tarumã trees, figs, pomegranates. Fruits in abundance. One thing intrigued the residents of Pedra Canga:

"How come all that if they don't sell it, give it away, or eat it?"

The fruits ripened, fell to the ground, rotted without being touched. An insult! Especially when you took into account the fact that the majority of people in Pedra Canga were poor, with many children, whose family income was barely enough for their daily rice and beans. Meat? A luxury. Only now and then. Greens and vegetables? Rare components of a meal. And there it was, right in front of everyone, that immense world of abundance that no one could touch. An outrage! Every time the neighborhood boys attempted an onslaught, they were rebuffed by salt pellets shot by unseen hands. Zigmundo, the bravest of them, had countless marks on his rear.

How many people lived in the big house? No one ever found out for sure. It appears that the population of the house consisted of four living creatures: Mr. V., his wife Leocádia Jacobina, and two servants, Nivalda and Nastácio.

Mr. V. took care of everything himself, assisted only by Nastácio, who was said to have been born a slave at the time of Colonel Totonho. He had never left the estate except at the orders of its owners. Silent and unsmiling, he was occasionally seen at Pedro Gambá's general store having a bit of rum in the morning. The store was next to the Municipal Market where the fishermen shouted out the catch of the day:

"Fresh pacu, right here in my hand, lady. Want some?"

"Is it really fresh?"

"It's still kicking. Feel it."

"A mess of curimbatá. It's cheap. Enough to feed all those kids you got at home. You goin' to take it, mister?"

"I wish I could...."

"Look here. Look here. I got fresh pintado. Want a string of them, m'am?"

"Heavens no. What would I do with so much fish?"

Nastácio would go to the market to buy some fish for his master and take advantage of the opportunity to have a drink or two. He learned the latest news from the conversations of the fishermen, who were assiduous customers of the store, which they made into a meeting place for their daily commentaries. Nastácio listened more than he talked. What did he have to talk about? He'd always lived on the Mangueiral, didn't have a single friend, no experiences with women, much less adventures of any kind. Until very recently he had thought that the world consisted only of the Mangueiral, but from the fishermen's stories, the tales of wild and noisy parties at Genu's cabaret, he was becoming more and more fascinated by the unknown. So was that what life was–a daily risk, different things happening all the time? But he had always lived in the monotony of the estate and thought that having room and board, along with work from dawn to dusk, was all there was. He never needed anything more than that. But now he was awakening to something new, something he still didn't understand but surely had to do with the nights of insomnia when he tossed in his hammock without finding a position that would allow him to sleep. Maybe the answer to everything lay in those talks at the store. He didn't know how to ask questions because he had been taught that questioning was the same as displaying arrogance. Obey blindly and never ask why, however absurd the order might be. Never argue with the master's orders. Even his own origin was unknown to him and he did not dare ask. He knew that his parents had been slaves of Colonel Totonho's, that his mother's name was Crescência; he didn't know his father's name but it didn't matter. He was dead, wasn't he? Would it do any good?

Years later I asked Maria Belarmina if she knew anything about Nastácio.

"I don't rightly know everything. What I do know's what I heard from Marcola, a horrifying story," she replied with a mysterious air.

"You can just stop repeating those stories of Marcola's," Neco Silvino interrupted, back from fishing. "She's getting senile and there's times when she can't make head nor tail of things."

Maria Belarmina replied angrily, "You're the one who's getting senile, you old fool. My friend is still very lucid. And don't forget that Marcola and me are about the same age. Are you by any chance trying to get at me?"

I didn't hear Neco Silvino's answer. I left the couple in the middle of that eternal prattle between husband

and wife after 40 years of marriage. I'm sure they didn't note my absence, given their involvement in the argument that, if nothing else, served to break the monotony of their long years together.

That same afternoon I decided to ask Marcola herself. I found her at her shack beside the Coxipó river, early the next morning, squatting in the doorway, drinking guaraná–a local custom that the old folks clung to like a religion; some called it "my vice." My grandfather Zé Garbas used to say, "If I don't have my guaraná in the morning, I'm no good for the rest of the day."

They said it was good for the heart, acting like a kind of elixir of longevity. Teodorico Metelo was pointed out as proof of the product's efficacy. He was over a hundred, a strong, active, and lucid old man: "And don't forget that as a young man I ate the devil's bread. I was a slave at Three Spears plantation and was 50 when I left there, at Emancipation. Or was that when it was?"

He didn't recollect all that well. But does it matter? The fact is that one day he became a free man, as free as a bird.

"C'mere, young lady. Want to hear a story about the time of slavery?" He had the habit of asking this of any pretty girl who passed his small thatch-roofed adobe house, at the corner of Lavradio street.

Marcola looked at me without surprise, as if she had been expecting me.

"Let's sit. It's a good day for confabulating."

She began to cut some tobacco for her pipe. She asked if I wanted to smoke. I thanked her but said I didn't smoke.

"But won't young missy at least have a bit of guaraná?" she asked in an affectionate tone.

How could I refuse? I knew it was very important to Marcola, and I myself would feel more at ease to begin our chat. It was a kind of ritual that would put us on the same plane. Speaker and listener using the same code to arrive at a clearer understanding of the facts.

I drank the guaraná slowly while quietly observing Marcola in her silence. I couldn't tell what age she was. Black, thin, tall, wearing a full skirt, colored beads, a white kerchief on her head, an embroidered blouse, a proud carriage–a forceful presence that both attracted and left a deep impression at the first instant.

Marcola seemed to be watching the flow of the river, but her eyes penetrated more than the river, more than the thick growth on its banks, more than Santo Antônio hill. They went further than my own eyes could reach. I tried but failed to keep pace with Marcola's gaze, so deeply buried in some world that my awareness could never attain.

"Missy came to find out about Nastácio, right? I was expecting missy," Marcola said gently.

I felt a sensation of immense peace at the side of that strange woman who could read my thoughts. I didn't need to introduce the matter and thus the brief speech that I had rehearsed, as a way to begin the talk, proved useless. She knew everything and was prepared.

"I'll start at the beginning. Missy can write in her little notebook whatever she thinks is important. If she needs more explaining, she can ask me to stop and I'll go back in time and search my memory better so's not to leave anything in doubt from forgetfulness."

I accepted the terms. I settled myself more comfortably on the stool she had provided for me to sit on, and anxiously awaited her words.

She closed her eyes and remained motionless for such a long time that I thought she had forgotten me. I didn't know what to do. I lacked the courage to break that silence, but my anxiety was such that I was nervously beginning to scribble my notes, when I heard Marcola's voice clearly:

"It's not going to work. My Guides haven't given me permission to talk today. Come back some other day."

"Come on, Miguelito! You're not gonna go back on your word this time," yelled Zigmundo, the leader of the group.

"Leave it to me, boss," answered Miguelito, with the posture of a recruit chosen for the platoon's first important mission.

Although he was twelve, no one would take him for more than eight. Tiny, with thin legs, the only thing large about him was his belly.

"He eats a lot of dirt, he's full of worms," said Expedito, another boy of the same age, who was considered the "brains" of the group, though it was unclear whether this was due to his ideas or the size of his head–so disproportionate that the nickname given him fit perfectly: Helmet Head.

"Screw you," he would answer when anyone called him by his nickname.

But that was merely an initial protest, because once the nickname caught on, nothing could be done about it. He resigned himself and even began to feel that the nickname afforded him a certain prestige or, rather, a certain respect among his fellows, especially after what happened in a soccer game on the banks of the Saranzal. The kids gathered to play all afternoon. The teams alternated, there was no referee, a role taken by the owner of the ball. The game almost always ended in a melee because no one was willing to accept defeat.

"You thief of a referee, you sonofabitch!"

"Faggot, faggot, faggot," screamed the enraged cheering section.

"Up your mother's ass," replied the owner of the ball.

Well, in one of those pick-up games Helmet Head butted Toninho Fleetfoot head to head, with the result that Fleetfoot ended up in the hospital with a suspected skull fracture, while Helmet Head, unhurt and completely calm, didn't even get a headache.

The remaining members of the group–Chico, Zelito, Ângelo, Evilázio, João Gonçalo–weren't outstanding figures but their loyalty to the others was universally recognized. After all, a common bond united them: poverty. They all came from extremely poor families, were undernourished, and lived in mud shacks–many people, little food, no comfort, great suffering, no future.

These children ran free, left to their own devices. Their parents had to work and there was no one to leave them with. The older ones looked after the younger ones. They learned at an early age to fend for themselves. No one told them what to do. They did as they pleased, pursuing their fantasies. Whatever rules they followed were their own, created by themselves.

"We're together through thick and thin," Zigmundo, the leader, repeated constantly.

And nothing better to unite people than the presence of a common obstacle to overcome. In this case, the Mangueiral estate–a challenge that even a blind man could see.

"I don't know what they want with all that. They let the fruit rot on the tree. They don't eat it, they don't give it away, they don't sell it. It's a sin," said the midwife Felícia, Zigmundo's mother.

"It's meanness. It's just so everybody'll envy them and to flaunt their power. But one day all that's going to change," said Ezekiel the Hermit, a strange figure who lived in isolation on Sovaco hill but who came from time to time to have a drink at the Gimme More bar.

The people of Pedra Canga were not resigned to the Vergare family's arrogance. Manifested or not, their indignation was palpable, a feeling accumulated over years, growing in strength, increasing, disputing. How long would this go on, for God's sake?

"Men, today I got a better plan of attack than last time. It can't fail," Zigmundo said, looking at the rest of the group, all of whom hung on the leader's every word.

"Ok," he went on. "There's eight of us. We'll work in pairs and jump the estate wall in several places, everybody at once. I'd like to see how Mr. V. can catch all of us. Don't forget to take sacks for the fruit, all you can carry, then you tie 'em and throw 'em over the wall and get away as fast as you can. Ok?"

"Yeah, it all looks perfect, but Mr. V.'s gonna catch one of us. And everybody knows what that means: salt pellets in the ass," objected Miguelito.

Zigmundo wasn't happy with the aside. He surveyed Miguelito from head to toe and said, "That's how come I called your attention to it at the start. You were the cause of our failure last time."

"Me?" Miguelito protested. "How's it my fault that Mr. V. has a pact with Old Nick? He's everywhere at once. It's like there's a hundred of him or he can read our minds."

"Don't talk drivel, Miguelito. We just gotta be faster'n him, that's all."

Then he stuck out his chest and shouted, "Let's go, guys! Quick. Last one there's a rotten coward."

And so the apprentice warriors marched off straight into the landowners' ambush. Mr. V. truly did seem to have a pact with the Horned One, for the estate was huge but he always showed up at the exact point of attack. This time it was no different. One salt-pellet after another pelted the panting, fleeing boys. But one or another of them managed something out of the adventure. Evilázio, for example, despite being small and bandy-legged, was jubilant upon his return, showing off a few ripe mangoes and an armful of pitombas.

"Pure luck," said Ângelo.

"No such thing," said João Gonçalo. "Evilázio is like greased lightning."

"You think he runs faster than Chico? I don't believe it."

Everyone was surprised at the vehemence of Ângelo, who was always quiet, in control, and never given to criticizing the behavior of a comrade.

"It's not going to work. Come back some other day." Marcola's words pounded inside my head for weeks. But what day, after all, was "some other day"? I preferred to wait for my intuition to give me a sign. And so it was. I arose early that morning of August 24; I remember it as if it were today, not only because the heat was unbearable, but also because it was my birthday. And can anyone forget her own birthday? Can they?

"Yes, they can," said my brother Luiz. "There's João Paduia, our neighbor. Every year we have to remind him."

"That's true," I agreed, a little miffed at having been shown up by my kid brother.

I set out for Marcola's house, this time without pencil or paper. Nothing. All I took was myself. I only wanted to talk to the woman and let things follow their own flow, accompanying the rhythm of the wind, though I knew there was no wind because the leaves on the trees were motionless.

"Hello, missy. Come on in." Marcola received me with a smile, standing at the door of her tiny shack, at the same time pointing toward an aged stool:

"Sit down. Sit here in the shade. It's so hot today...."

She went inside and returned with a pitcher of tamarind juice and two aluminum mugs.

"Would missy like some?"

"Please. Thank you very much."

Raising the glass above her head, Marcola offered a toast for my birthday:

"May your life be sunny like an August day and may your eyes see the many paths written on the leaves of the palms.

"May the green murity palm spread oil on your feet so the ground you tread will never be rough.

"May the white heron of the Lowlands show you the nest of light where the song of life knows no sunset.

"Blessed be the force that brought you into the world, missy!"

Her words were like a shower of energy falling on my skin. I freed myself, became a gentle wind blowing between the pines, and went to play among the sweet fragrance of the flowering tarumã trees.

"Something more to drink?" Marcola's voice summoned me back.

"Yes. It's quite good. Thank you very much."

"Today I woke up remembering Crescência. She died

in the month of August, but I can't remember what day." Marcola began to talk, looking at the motionless leaves of the trees.

I wanted to interrupt and ask who Crescência was, but something inside held me back and I decided to listen in silence. Marcola continued:

"She was Colonel Totonho's slave. A proud, pretty girl with a fine figure, who liked to show herself off. She was taken from the slave quarters to serve as personal maid to Dona Sinhazinha, the colonel's wife. Young Crescência was the same age as Mr. V., and wouldn't you know that they fell in love? The result was that Mr. V. got Crescência pregnant and had the audacity to tell his father he wanted to marry her. It was a scandal. Colonel Totonho was furious and sent Mr. V. to a boarding school in the state capital. Crescência went back to the slave quarters, dying from grief and mistreatment soon after the child was born. Dona Sinhazinha took the newborn into the house, baptised him with the name Nastácio, and the poor man is still there to this very day, serving as slave to his own father and not knowing anything. Isn't that perverse?" Marcola concluded, looking deeply into my eyes.

I saw a flame of hatred flaring in her eyes. She sprang up abruptly, with the agility of a young girl, ran to the middle of the courtyard, and, pointing in the direction of the river, screamed, "Yes, but it will not remain this way. Divine justice may be long in coming but is never denied. Those wicked people will pay for all the evil they did. And it will be in this life, for hell is right here."

Surprised at the tone of Marcola's words, I looked at her, trying to discover where so much rage was coming from. I froze inside. Marcola was no longer Marcola. Her face was completely transformed. In the place of her wrinkled cheeks, her fallen lips, her serene expression, was another face–young, pretty, full of life, angry–demanding vengeance.

Not knowing what to do, I couldn't take my eyes off the strange woman whose identity I no longer knew. I watched as she sat down, picked up a twig and scratched in the dirt a word that, with great difficulty, I managed to read: CRESCÊNCIA.

Some time later I met Marcola at the Municipal Market and she asked:

"When is missy coming back to my house so we can talk? I've been waiting all this time. I promised I'd tell you the story of Nastácio, remember?"

Maria Belarmina, rosary in hand, asked for protection from Our Lady of Deliverance on the night of the tempest.

"My patron saint, don't let us perish. We cannot pay for a sin we didn't commit."

"That's right, my friend. This is heaven's punishment for Mr. V., a dev–I mean, the Evil One incarnate," Felícia said in support.

"Just like his father, Colonel Totonho, that scourge, that monster of iniquity," Maria Belarmina said, ending the conversation.

My father told me that the owners of the Mangueiral had always had power and wealth. Boundless territory in the lowlands, cattle, and countless slaves, but people said that it had all been "badly come by." As an example they spoke of the case of the rancher Nicolau Paranhos, an extremely rich man from Nhecolândia, who overnight lost everything he had to the Vergares.

"The poor man was left with nothing but the clothes on his back; he couldn't take the setback, went crazy and died in the São Sebastião Asylum. His relatives and friends took no notice."

I asked how the Vergares had managed to take away the rancher's lands, and my father told me it had been very simple because Nicolau Paranhos didn't know how to read or write, only how to sign his name. So the Vergares drew up the papers and asked their friend to sign, making up some story or other.

"In all confidence, Paranhos signed, not knowing he was signing over everything he owned to the Vergares. At least that's how I heard the story," my father concluded.

Uncle Mário entered the conversation to say that he also had heard horrible things, and that reputedly Colonel Totonho's wickedness knew no limits.

"They say he used to punish his slaves for any reason at all, for the simple pleasure of seeing them suffer. He killed runaway slaves by beating them to death and by other tortures, especially by starvation and letting them die of thirst."

"That's right," my mother interrupted, to my surprise. "But through God's punishment he died of a strange disease, with his throat in flames, attacked by a thirst that no water would quench. He became a soul in torment and has haunted any number of people who risk walking along the riverbank in the dead of night."

At this point my father fell silent. When it came to things of the other world, as he said, "I don't believe it and I don't disbelieve it, but I do respect it."

Hortência Flores, the clairvoyant, known and respected throughout Pedra Canga, declared she had seen Colonel Totonho's soul pursued by a band of souls of the slaves he had murdered.

"He will not find rest until he pays for his crimes," affirmed the clairvoyant.

Maria Belarmina clung to her rosary and asked Neco Silvino not to look out the window anymore. It was the end of the world. The Foul Fiend was on the loose, the only hope was to pray. Lightning bolts, stronger each time, seemed bent on setting the earth on fire. The whistling wind brought sounds of fury and desperation. Suddenly there was a knock at the door.

"Don't open it. It's Death trying to get in," Maria Belarmina screamed at her husband.

"Stop talking foolishness, woman. It must be somebody who needs help."

He opened the door and sprang back in fright when a disheveled woman, the image of terror, with her one good eye almost leaping from its socket, said:

"Help me, for the love of God. My master is dying and the house has been taken over by horrible people who're carrying out a blood ceremony. They tried to kill me but I got away. I don't have anywhere to go and I'm scared to death. Can I stay here? Can I?"

Neco Silvino felt a shiver run through him. He couldn't speak. He had seen the woman before. She

39

was Nivalda, the Vergares' servant. How could he forget? The scene of the bonfire leapt vividly into his memory, burning his brain, paralyzing him.

With sudden courage, Maria Belarmina went up to Nivalda and ordered her to leave. Crossing herself, she expelled the wretched woman and securely locked and bolted the door:

"By the Cross I cast you out. Vade retro Satanas."

Neco Silvino did not react to his wife's attitude. He felt lost, lacking the strength to take control of matters. What a night, and no sign of morning! As a child he had heard stories of how the world would end. He would fall asleep huddled against his mother's ribs, asking God to let him sleep soundly. He wanted to be sleeping when the world came to an end. But now he was wide awake, a grown man, his mother was dead, and he didn't know how to control the sequence of strange things that were happening right under his nose. Could this be the end of the world? Was this the way the world would come to an end? The sounds from the Mangueiral grew and became louder than the storm.

"Mother, wherever you are, don't abandon your son at this hour," the fisherman prayed softly.

"NIVALDA, THE EVIL WITCH. Glass-eyed Nivalda. Goat's-hoof Nivalda" was the chant of the boys who followed Nivalda every time she appeared in the street on errands for her masters.

The boys gave her no respite, and to make matters worse, threw stones and sicked dogs on her. Nivalda, a tall, skinny mulatto woman with long legs, a missing eye, and a large scar right in the middle of her left cheek, did indeed have a strange appearance, but she had never done evil to anyone. Why did they persecute her so? Perhaps because she lived on the Mangueiral and thus was an easy target for the boys who mistreated her as revenge for the abuse they received at the hands of Mr. V.; I don't know. Or perhaps it was because of the stories they heard about Nivalda from their parents. Miguelito, Neco Silvino's grandson, had heard his grandfather recount the episode of the "witchcraft" night. Quite impressed, he never forgot the part in which his grandfather declared he'd heard a woman screaming, "For the love of God, don't put out my eye!"

So, "since Nivalda is missing an eye, then it was her, and after that you can be sure she turned into a witch,"

Miguelito concluded, passing along the story to the rest of the group. Repeated with constant exaggeration, it went from mouth to mouth, growing in proportion until it reached the ears of the last to know–Chico, who said, his eyes bulging and mouth agape, "Holy Mary, you mean she's got a goat's hoof and a dragon's head and spouts fire out of her snout?"

"What snout, Chico? She's people just like we are."

"How can you be sure, Helmet Head?"

Felícia, the midwife, swore that she knew of Nivalda's origins. She said she had been a foundling who appeared along the edge of the river, on the Mangueiral bank, and the Vergares took her in to raise.

"But she was brought up as a slave. They always mistreated her badly, and the poor woman was punished and beaten every day," Felícia emphasized.

She also said that Nastácio had told her that one day Mr. V. struck her in the face so hard that her eye came out of its socket.

"What about that horrible mark on her face, isn't it a birthmark, the sign of somebody who's cursed?" Maria Belarmina asked.

"You're wrong," said Marcola, who arrived in time to catch the end of the conversation. "What happened was that Dona Jacobina, in a fit of rage, threw a pan of boiling water in the poor woman's face. Anyone can see it's the sign of an ugly burn."

"I don't know," Maria Belarmina continued. "Who can prove it was hot water and not a burn from hellfire, which is where she came from?"

In my view, she was nothing but a poor frightened child who had never known kindness, the victim of cruelty from birth.

On the night Mr. V. lay dying, after she was driven away by Maria Belarmina, Nivalda found herself alone in the midst of the storm, with nowhere to go. She knocked at doors, begged for help, but no one heard, or they pretended not to hear. Finally, soaked to the bone, her teeth chattering from cold and fear, she came to Genu's cabaret, the only place in Pedra Canga open at that time of night.

Genu? Who didn't know Genu? A slight woman with a sharp glance, craggy hands that looked like claws, braver than anyone, she was reputed to have shooed away many a macho male and had run the Open Heaven for over 15 years. The house boasted the fine services of six young women blindly obedient to Genu, whose motto was "A satisfied customer will come again." Genu took great pride in her "girls," as she liked to call them. She didn't allow them to work in the kitchen or clean the house. That was forbidden.

"I have two servants for the heavy work. I don't want my girls ruining their nails, because their work is high-level and demands an impeccable appearance.

My clientele has class"—even though the customers were fishermen, truck drivers, soldiers, stevedores, and rubber tappers.

"So what? They have class, since it's in bed that you see what a man's upbringing is," said Genu in defense.

The Open Heaven cabaret did so well that Genu had a neon sign put up over the entrance, with the word OPEN in yellow letters and HEAVEN in blue letters, not to mention an enormous heart pierced by a bright red arrow, no less, the symbol of true love. But the naysayers commented that whoever drew it either had a dirty mind or was a terrible artist, for it wasn't a heart at all but a plump and inviting fanny, and the arrow looked more like a stiff cock. But woe to anyone who even skirted the subject with Genu. The diminutive woman would turn purple with wrath.

"They want to throw mud on my house, but my conscience is what matters. I had him draw a heart and an arrow representing Cupid, the god of love. Whoever doesn't understand either the drawing or my intention are dirty-minded ignoramuses. Fuck 'em and they can shove it up their ass! You ladies and gentlemen will forgive my irritation," she normally concluded her "impromptu" speech, usually on Friday night when the house was packed and she'd had a little too much to drink. Everyone would applaud and excited shouts of "Genu's got class!" would fill the air,

44

sometimes punctuated by some newcomer who tried his hand at rhyme—"Show us your ass! Show us your ass!"—but was quickly silenced by the others.

"More respect, buddy. You ain't talking to your mother."

The guy caught the drift, stuck his tail between his legs, and got into the spirit of the house.

One day someone went further: "Who's this Cupid? Somebody who died from a stopped-up ass?" But his voice was lost amid the laughter and the beer flowing to the sound of the victrola playing a Paraguayan polka very popular at the time, "Mis noches sin ti."

Another rule of the house: Genu demanded absolute secrecy about what went on at the cabaret.

"Here people's privacy is respected. What goes on between a man and a woman, only the walls know. Nobody else. Nobody asks questions when the customer arrives or when he leaves. If he wants to talk about his life, that's his business, but none of the girls is going to spread around what she heard from his mouth. That I can guarantee or my name isn't Genu."

Nivalda finally found an open door. Maybe in this house full of people she could find shelter.

"Help me, for the love of God," she moaned, almost fainting.

In the commotion someone called Genu, who as usual was in her office doing the bookkeeping.

"Genu, come quick. There's a crazy woman here who must've escaped from the asylum, and we don't know what to do."

Genu dashed to the middle of the parlor, where she found Nivalda in the condition that the reader is already aware of but which was a shock for the cabaret owner.

"My God, what're you doing here at this hour, Nivalda?"

"My master is dying and the house's been taken over by horrible people performing blood rituals. They tried to kill me but I got away. I don't have anywhere to go and I'm afraid. Can I stay here? Can I?"

"What kind of talk is that? Who's that woman? Throw 'er out," said a voice in the midst of the confusion.

"Shut up! Keep your nose out of this. I run things here," Genu replied. "I know this poor woman and know very well what she's talking about. I'll do what needs to be done. Get back to the party. I'll take her inside and everything'll be all right."

Thus was Nivalda's hasty passage through Genu's parlor. From then on she spent all her time in the kitchen, working from sunrise to sunset in exchange for food and used clothing from the "girls." Her existence went unnoticed in the whirlwind that was Open Heaven.

A SUNNY DAY, a blue sky, birds singing, the good smell of moist earth, everything contributing to a perfect contrast with what had happened the night before. But what actually *had* happened? Everyone had a different experience to recount to his neighbor, and the various stories quickly went from mouth to mouth.

No one could explain to me that morning how the rumor began. How did they learn of Mr. V.'s death? No one knew who had begun spreading the news, but many affirmed that he had died. The more reticent among them said, "It seems like he died" or "Everything points to him being dead." I asked Maria Belarmina how she found out.

"Somebody told me," she said drily.

I went looking for Felícia, who had been Dona Sinhazinha's midwife when Mr. V. was born, and she said, "I was the first to touch the newborn's body. My hands don't feel that he's dead. Or at least he didn't die of natural causes. Something took him, body and all, to some place. He was swallowed whole."

At that point I thought that the only person who could provide some clarification was Marcola, who,

47

coincidentally, was arriving at Felícia's house just as I was leaving.

"If he's dead, where's the body and when will the funeral be?" I asked.

Marcola looked deep into my eyes and replied, "You speak of body and death as if you knew what happened," and continued on her way, leaving me in the dark about her meaning.

"Well, did he die or didn't he?" I shouted as I saw her disappearing into the distance.

She turned around and said, "There are things in this world that our understanding is too limited to grasp."

I still didn't know.

The entire neighborhood was talking about the death of Mr. V., how it happened, how it didn't happen, in a mixture of curiosity and indignation:

"What kind of people don't even have the decency to let folks in Pedra Canga know about Mr. V.'s death?"

Maria Belarmina told me, "As far as I'm concerned, they can hide the death any way they want to, but one thing's for sure: He has to be buried, doesn't he? Well then. Everybody's going to see it when the funeral procession comes by."

She was right. The Seven Guardians of the Sand cemetery was located on Faraway Hill, and the only way there was along Gravel street, smack in the middle of Pedra Canga.

Since Mr. V. had died at night, even if the exact time was unknown, in keeping with tradition the procession would have to pass through there no later than five in the afternoon. From three on, people began gathering along Gravel street. No one wanted to miss the slightest detail of the funeral. They wanted to see the coffin, the widow's face, the servants Nivalda and Nastácio, and anyone else who might be accompanying the procession.

At five on the dot the funeral cortege appeared at the beginning of the street. To everyone's surprise, no one had ever seen such a large procession. In their great curiosity, they could hardly wait for the moment when they would see everything up close. Where had all those people come from?

"As best I know, nobody here in Pedra Canga was invited," Maria Belarmina said.

"And like everybody knows, they don't have friends. They never went anywhere and nobody ever visited them," added Mané Pitchpenny, who owned the Gimme More.

"I heard he has a lot of family around Corumbá," commented Jandira Meireles, owner of the Empty Basket bakery.

"You're wrong," answered Maria Belarmina. "Mr. V. has just one son, who's a bachelor and only thinks about partying. He travels all the time all over the place, and at the moment his whereabouts is unknown. In fact, nobody rightly knows if he's dead or alive."

Someone requested silence. The procession was passing by. Surprise was universal: There were more than a hundred people, all dressed in black. Strangers. Women with veils covering their heads and part of their faces. Men in dark glasses, long beards, and black felt hats, walking rapidly toward the cemetery. No one saw the coffin, or any sign of the widow or the servants. Smoking Snake, the town drunk, strongly disputed this last statement:

"So you don't think I'm anybody, huh? Well, for your information I was there at the cemetery when the procession arrived. I saw the coffin and it was open. A big guy was carrying the cover. I looked inside the coffin and saw Mr. V.'s body inside there, stiff as a board. I couldn't see his face because he didn't have a head. They buried the body without a head."

The vehement testimony of Smoking Snake fell like a hurricane among the people, shaking structures and provoking strong reactions. "Who's going to believe that depraved alcoholic?" asked Ludovica.

"I believe him," my grandfather Zé Garbas replied. "As far as I'm concerned, he saw it and that's all there is to it. What difference does it make if he was drunk or not? Maybe that's why he could stand seeing what he did."

Of one thing everyone was certain: Smoking Snake spent most of his time at the cemetery; often he even slept there, and he made a point of being present at every funeral, even when he didn't know the deceased.

"So, did Mr. V. die or didn't he?" Maria Belarmina asked her husband Neco Silvino.

"Beats me. How should I know? Some say he did, others say he didn't."

"That's a good one!" Maria Belarmina retorted. "You *should* know. You spend all your time with those foul-mouthed booze hounds at the Gimme More who talk about everybody and his brother. I never get out of the house. I'm here all day long working like a slave and don't have time to go around asking about things."

"Is that right?" Neco Silvino answered. "Be careful with all those lies, God is listening. You don't do nothing but gossip with the neighbors."

"At least I do something. That's better than your sister Pulquéria who sits around on her ass and tells everybody how hard she works washing clothes. Ha! Ha! Ha!"

I don't know why I've transcribed this unenlightening argument about the strange and much discussed death of Mr. V. The pair continued fighting for the rest of the morning and in all likelihood didn't even recall the cause of the commotion.

Why didn't I think of going to the Gimme More? Well, that's exactly what I did. On the way, I remembered that the first time I went into the bar had been at the wedding of Benvinda Flor, Mané Pitchpenny's oldest daughter. A rollicking, noisy party. Practically the whole neighborhood showed up, and since the father of the bride was none other than the owner of the famous bar, what everyone was waiting for came to pass: free drinks for one and all.

I took advantage of the opportunity. I had to. It was the only chance for a woman to go into the bar and not be "talked about" in the entire town. Or so I thought, but I quickly discovered I was totally mistaken. Not everyone was tying one on that day. My presence was noted, registered, and commented upon even by Ezekiel the Hermit, as soon as the hubbub about the wedding had settled down. *Note*: I forgot to mention that the bride was four months pregnant when she got married and, according to Ludovica Hosteater, "getting married wearing white in 'that condition' was a sacrilege, a mortal sin." It was a scandal to the parishioners of St. Gonçalo's church, who were unflagging in their condemnation of Celestial Archangel, the mother of the bride: "With a mother like that, what could you expect?"

Well, all that was nothing compared to my rapid incursion into the bar.

"Since when does a self-respecting young lady set foot in a place for men only? It's shameless. What's she after? You can be sure she's no virgin any more," said Ludovica.

Someone came to my defense: "Says who? I don't see anything wrong with a woman coming into a bar and having a drink or two. What's virginity got to do with it? Or to put it in plain language, don't confuse shit with Shinola."

Who was that someone? the uninformed may ask. Who else could it be? Smoking Snake. With such a feeble defender, it might be expected that my cause was doomed from the start. And so it was. My name went on the list of those whose classification varied from crazy to "hopeless sinner."

There was, I recall, another voice raised in my favor: "She's a writer and she's gathering facts to write a novel," said a voice that I never succeeded in recognizing.

Would it have done any good? The voice was quickly supplanted by Ludovica: "She's no writer. Just because she carries around that black notebook everywhere she goes? Pretense, nothing but pretense. Who knows what she's writing? You can be sure it's something indecent."

My friend Marilza Ribeiro, the famous poet of Pedra Canga, came to my defense and tried to dialogue with Ludovica, but the latter categorically refused, saying she had no desire to converse with people of our "ilk."

After a certain time the comments began cooling down and I came to be seen by the community as "extravagant," "different," "odd." And, as always happens in small towns, they forgot about me as soon as a new topic came along: the death of Mr. V. No one in Pedra Canga talked about anything else. So much so that, on the morning of August 25–Armed Forces Day–I headed calmly for the Gimme More without encountering so much as a suspicious glance or reproachful stare along the way.

At the bar I found Big Tomás. I had a drink with him while he listened to country music on the radio– "The Death of Chico Mineiro," a lachrymose story about the death of a cattle herder. I ordered a second drink, and while I waited for Mané Pitchpenny to prepare the "specialty of the house," was startled to see everyone in the bar draw back in fright and point to the door:

"It's the witch! It's the witch!"

"Who?" I asked Big Tomás, apparently the calmest person among the customers.

"Don't you see her?" he said. "It's Nivalda, the Vergares' servant. She'd disappeared and here she is back again. I wonder what she wants."

I looked at the tiny, tremulous, wizened creature, her gaze fixed on the floor as she moved rapidly toward the counter and said in a low voice, "My boss lady Genu sent me here for two bottles of rum and asked you to put it on her account."

"All right," muttered Mané Pitchpenny. "Take the bottles and get out of my sight, you devil's spawn."

Nivalda took the bottles and dashed out of the bar.

To this day I don't know what came over me. I ran out after her and called her: "Nivalda, Nivalda, wait a minute, I want to talk to you."

She stopped, looked at me with her one good eye, and said, "My boss Genu told me not to talk to strangers. Everybody hates me and wants to hurt me."

"I don't hate you, Nivalda," I replied, "and I don't want to hurt you. All I want is to talk to you."

"What for? What do you want to know–if I'm really a witch? Is that it? Well, you can go to hell too." And she continued on her way toward Open Heaven.

I tried unsuccessfully to follow her. She went into the cabaret and closed the door. I stood there for a time trying to figure out the reason behind my gesture, angry at myself because in the final analysis I saw no difference between me and the people who mistreated Nivalda. I thought about her words and asked myself what *did* I want with her? I discovered that, deep down, it was mere curiosity, opportunism, the search for material to continue this narrative. I had no feeling of solidarity or respect in me when I approached her. She saw through me and fled.

Helmet Head was the first to have the idea of probing the Vergares' orchard. After all, it was now seven days since Mr. V. had died, and he thought that after the Mass of the seventh day, no one was obliged to go on mourning for a guy as bad as he was.

"There wasn't any Mass," said Miguelito. And no one doubted him because he was an altar boy at St. Gonçalo's and helped Father Guilhermino with everything having to do with Mass, baptisms, weddings, and prayers.

"So what're we waiting for? Let's round up the rest of the gang and get going," said João Gonçalo.

"Right," Chico agreed. In less than a half hour they were all gathered beneath the old fig tree in the center of Market Square.

Zigmundo, the leader, laid out an infallible plan as always: They would enter the Mangueiral through the rear, along the banks of the Saranzal. Normally this would be a very risky plan because of the alligators, but as it was dry season the river formed a small beach and the animals remained at a distance, in the water. The group silently followed their chief. Zigmundo went

57

first and squatted under the sarandi trees, where he remained for a long time staring at the large old house to see if anyone appeared. Nothing. Everything closed up, quiet. No sign of life about. He whistled and the group joined him. Zigmundo said, "Every man for himself from here on. Grab what you can and light out for all you're worth."

"Right," and each went off in a different direction in search of any kind of ripe fruit. Or even green fruit.

It was a success. Everyone grabbed as much as he wanted. They ran back to the square, each one proudly exhibiting the day's harvest: guavas, mangoes, oranges, starfruit.

"I don't understand anything," said Miguelito, who, like the others, was used to persecution from the owners of the Mangueiral and had no explanation for such tranquility.

"Yeah, but Mr. V.'s dead," Evilázio reminded him.

Zelito interrupted, saying that wasn't the reason, 'cause where were the rest of the people in the house? And the dogs?

"Now that you mention it, I didn't even see the alligators," said Ângelo, always formal.

They sensed that something strange was happening, but they didn't give the matter any further thought. The important thing at the moment was to enjoy the fruit, so ripe it made their mouths water.

The news spread that same day: The Mangueiral estate was deserted. Where had Dona Jacobina and Nastácio gone? And what about Salustiano Vergare, Mr. V.'s only child, who was said to have arrived from Corumbá at the last minute to attend his father's funeral?

"I'm sure the fellow arrived," said Neco Silvino. According to him, Mário the Pirate, a childhood friend, had come on the same boat as the Mangueiral heir.

"But he didn't show up at the funeral," Maria Belarmina said.

Neco Silvino shrugged as if to indicate that he too understood nothing more. Suddenly, he jumped, turned to Maria Belarmina and pointed his finger right at her nose:

"How do you know he wasn't at the funeral? You don't know him...."

Maria Belarmina muttered something like "Go to hell!" and left hurriedly.

"Neco, they're saying that Salustiano Vergare chartered a plane and took his father's body to be buried in the family mausoleum in Corumbá, and that Dona Jacobina went with him," said Pulquéria, entering the conversation as soon as she arrived at her brother's house.

"What about Nastácio? What happened to him?" Neco Silvino asked.

"Some people are saying he ran away so as not to go with the masters. Others say he got on the plane with the Vergares. Chico Nepomuceno is telling everybody that Nastácio is safe and sound, living with the fishermen upriver, happy as can be. I don't know. All's I know is that the estate's abandoned."

That night the news spread even further. Passing freely from house to house, it transcended the limits of Pedra Canga, as far as Barro Fundo, Despraiado, Várzea Grande, growing like a river current. No one could hold it back. I became lost in the search for its movements, tried to seize it by the tail when it swept by me, but was unable even to keep up with the effects its rumbling occasioned wherever it passed.

The next morning the adults decided to go with the boys on an exploratory mission to the Mangueiral. Maria Belarmina, Felícia, Pulquéria, Neco Silvino, Big Tomás, and many others that didn't register in my memory. I remember one person who didn't go: my mother. She thought it was something that crazy people did and that no one had the right to trespass on other people's land, though Luíza Branquinha had tried to convince her that the interlopers were the Vergares when they took the lands of Antônio dos Anjos. My mother insisted she knew nothing about that story, but she was sure of one thing: "What those people are doing just isn't right."

Guided by the boys, they cautiously entered the Mangueiral. They crossed the grassy courtyard, full of coconut trees and Acrocomia palms squarely in front of the house. They knocked at the door, once, twice, three times. No answer. They went around the house and tried at the back door. Nothing. Suddenly, they heard a savage scream and the sound of dragging chains coming from the second floor:

"Who dares to invade my lands?"

No one waited to see whose voice it was. They got out of there as fast as they could, except for Big Tomás, who stood there paralyzed, his legs refusing to move. He remembered what his father had told him when he confronted the werewolf, and terror possessed him completely. Neco Silvino had to pull him away, by fits and starts.

"The mulatto's feet were like they were made of lead, glued to the ground," the fisherman said.

When she learned of the retinue's debacle, my mother said between clinched teeth, "May Our Lady of Guidance save us. I for one am not going to that cursed place. Not me, not my children."

My grandfather Zé Garbas took advantage of the opportunity to attack Neco Silvino once again: "Who? That coward? I'll bet my life he didn't hear anything. He runs away for no reason and shits his pants."

And the theme was later used in one of his famous songs:

Neco Silvino, what was it now?
A hissing cat or a mooing cow?
Stop your lies, you cringing fart
Fear's all you carry in your heart
There's no ghosts at the estate
So stop your lying before it's too late.

But some said that Big Tomás had confirmed the story, though in a different version:

"I didn't hear anybody's voice saying anything. What I heard was just a bellow as loud as thunder. Even the ground shook."

Maria Belarmina would neither confirm nor deny. She recalled quite well that her hair had stood on end and she'd felt a chill in the pit of her stomach–signs that, for her, could only be a warning that something from the other world was nearby.

Pulquéria was rather evasive and said, "This is nothing to mess around with," then changed the subject when pressed for further details.

Felícia was categorical: "Well, nobody's going to fool me. That was Mr. V.'s voice. I caught the wretch when he came into the world and I heard his first screams. It was him, it was him," she repeated incessantly.

The people of Pedra Canga had no reason to doubt Felícia, although some, like Luíza Branquinha, didn't understand how she could make a connection between the bellow of a monster and the innocent cry of a newborn. Marcola said that she agreed completely with Felícia, because according to her, Mr. V. had been born with an evil spirit and surely hadn't cried like an ordinary baby. Besides that, Felícia was considered a reasonable person, a woman of substance–not only because she weighed 250 pounds but also because her word weighed heavily in the scales of decision. Whenever a difficult dispute arose, in which the parties couldn't reach agreement, Felícia was called on for her view.

"And she always found the best solution," said Maria Belarmina. She proceeded to tell of the case of the seven piglets, in which Felícia's decision was incontestable.

She told me the case had become famous and had even reached Italy, carried by Brazilian soldiers who participated in the Second World War.

"Just between us, a case talked about by the heroes of Monte Castello has to be important, doesn't it?"

I confessed to knowing nothing about the seven piglets, and she seemed rather disappointed.

The next day I sought out Felícia and found out about the case. From beginning to end.

LUDOVICA HOSTEATER lived by herself in a large old house with many bedrooms, parlors, and hallways. Walls covered with family photographs, from her great-grandfather Clementino Josué Cravo to her parents Armandina and Hipólito Cravo, were her company. An only child, she had survived the bubonic plague that had wiped out the Cravo family. Alone, an old maid and a virgin, over fifty, she had no alternative: She dedicated herself body and soul to religion. She never left the church. She confessed and took communion every Sunday at six o'clock Mass and was an active member of the Daughters of Mary Sisterhood. Founder of the Closed Circle of Morality and Decency–whose purpose was to maintain close vigilance over the purity of the damsels of Pedra Canga–Ludovica added one more frustration to her life: The Circle was disbanded for lack of followers. She blamed the weekly dances at the Flaming Cock honky-tonk, on Gaslight Alley–a den of perdition that led young women away from the path of virtue and modesty.

"A sign of the times. Since when does a cheap little club like that hold such attraction for young people?

The dance floor is full of holes and the bathroom is like a pigsty."

To the surprise of the parishioners at St. Gonçalo's, this little speech was delivered in a loud voice on the steps of the church, on Sunday after nine o'clock Mass. Everyone heard it. Pulquéria, who was passing by at that moment, replied, "So, Hosteater, you've tried the Flaming Cock?"

Ludovica pretended she hadn't heard and continued talking on behalf of morality and decorum. She couldn't stop. Those were moments of glory for her. She managed to gather a few people around her, which in a way gave her the impression of not being alone in the world. But it was all so fast.... The small crowd moved away and she returned home to confront once again the agony of loneliness.

It was in one of those periods of total depression that Ludovica got the idea of raising a suckling pig. She spoke with Manoel Joaquim, who delivered milk every morning to her door, and he promised to look around for someone with a piglet for sale. Ludovica corrected the milkman, saying she wanted a clean little suckling, healthy and demonstrably virgin. Manoel Joaquim realized he had a difficult mission before him.

"Man, is that one demanding bitch," he grumbled.

A week later the milkman appeared with the suckling wrapped in a burlap bag. Ludovica was very happy, paid him, and disappeared inside the house with measured steps as if she were carrying a newborn baby. The first thing was to bathe the suckling using a luxurious brand of soap. Fragrant and clean, with a metal tag around her neck bearing the name Fleur-de-Lis, the tiny animal grunted happily.

Hosteater cared for the suckling like an only daughter. She set aside a special place for her in the house and fed her three times a day. Fleur-de-Lis never went out to the back yard because Ludovica was afraid she would get dirty or catch a cold. With so much care, the suckling grew and fattened until she became, in the words of her owner, "a full-grown young woman." It's true that the size of Fleur-de-Lis's belly was a bit exaggerated, but Ludovica took two important factors into account: proper feeding and good care. And everything went well. She saw Fleur-de-Lis every day and no longer felt so alone.

One afternoon Ludovica received a visit from Jeová Salgado, the biggest pig farmer in the area. The reason for the visit almost killed her, because Salgado stated that Fleur-de-Lis was pregnant and that the author of the deed was a thoroughbred pig that he'd bought as a breeder and that, therefore, the offspring belonged to him, since the animal was his. Ludovica was thunderstruck and said that was impossible, it was slander, and that Fleur-de-Lis had never been in the yard and had never had contact with the opposite sex. Jeová Salgado retorted that it wasn't true, and if she wanted to go to the yard and check for herself she'd see there was a hole in the fence, where, probably, the suckling had squeezed through to rendezvous with his boar Wax Stick. Hosteater was firm on this point, saying that if by any chance it had happened, without a doubt it was that experienced and malicious boar's fault, not Fleur-de-Lis's.

"Whadya mean? I always keep my boar tied up in my yard!" Salgado roared furiously.

But she wouldn't hear of it. In any case, that wasn't the most important point. What emerged in the argument as a point of honor is that Ludovica declared that Fleur-de-Lis was a virgin and would brook no doubts about the fact until proven otherwise. That was when they decided to call on Felícia, the midwife, for the acid test.

Felícia arrived, carefully examined the suckling and answered categorically, "Fleur-de-Lis is a virgin."

"Didn't I say so?" said Ludovica triumphantly.

"But she's pregnant," Felícia added.

"Didn't I say so?" It was Salgado's turn.

Ludovica cried a lot but there was nothing she could do. Fleur-de-Lis had seven piglets and her owner gave them all to Jeová Salgado. She didn't even want to see the offspring, which she deemed the work of Satan. For her, Fleur-de-Lis was still the same pure and unstained suckling she had always been, for despite everything, she was still a virgin, even after the birth of the seven piglets, as had been confirmed by the midwife Felícia.

The only change noted in Fleur-de-Lis after the tragedy was a vague gaze, full of sadness and longing, that appeared from time to time on her pink snout.

THE BOYS went on jumping the estate fence, each day more at ease than the day before. Now they were certain no one would chase them. They took fruit at will. No one bothered them.

Then it was the older people's turn. If it was as easy as all that, why not take advantage of it? As they were no longer spry enough to leap over the wall, they decided to make a hole in it, which grew wider and wider until it became a door, then a gate, then a larger gate.

People came and went at all hours, always laden with fruit and vegetables. At first they chose only ripe fruits, but then the green ones as well: stalks of bananas, watermelons, starfruit, papayas, guavas, mangoes, oranges. They began to uproot the fields. For nothing. They cut down trees, bundled up the wood, placed it in hand barrows or wagons, then returned for more. I remember that our normally peaceful street became extremely busy, and because of its narrowness could barely handle the number of passersby.

Many strangers appeared, carrying off whatever they could. The residents of Pedra Canga were first, but the news spread through neighboring towns and then to others farther away, and people started coming from all directions. Sometimes entire families passed by with sacks or crates whose contents we could only guess.

They began arriving very early in the morning and didn't stop until nightfall. From my door I watched those people go by. They seemed like an anthill in their ceaseless movement. The speed with which they came and went made it seem as if they were stealing. Which in fact they were. More than that, they were swallowing up everything.

In two weeks they ate up the fruits, the vegetables, the herbs. Then they invaded the area of the livestock: chickens, turkeys, geese, ducks, pigs, goats. They didn't even spare some mongrels they chanced upon there, sniffing out something to eat. It seemed that everything they encountered on the estate was of priceless value. Maria Belarmina told me they even dug up paving stones:

"I think they're digging in hopes of finding gold. There can't be any other reason. If not, why would they go to all that trouble?"

They attacked the fences. They tore down fenceposts and rolled up the barbed wire. They destroyed the walls and obliterated the Mangueiral boundary lines from the ground.

They worked in silence. They walked with rapid

steps, heads lowered, in a rhythm that obeyed some unknown cadence. An invisible command seemed to drive them.

Who were they? Pulquéria told me she'd never seen any of them before. That gave me pause, for I was aware that she knew everyone for miles around. Smoking Snake said that, despite his not knowing those people, their faces were somehow familiar.

"What do you mean, familiar?" asked Mané Pitchpenny skittishly.

"They all have the face of the recently deceased that I see coming into the cemetery every day. Not a one of them has a drop of blood in their faces. Haven't you noticed?"

"For the love of God, Smoking Snake! Are you saying they're not of this world?" asked Mané Pitchpenny, frightened.

Smoking Snake threw back a shot of rum, hawked, spat, and said that he wasn't saying anything; he just saw a strange coincidence between the color of those creatures and that of dead people, and furthermore he'd never heard them speak.

"Have you heard a conversation, or laughter, or even a whisper, from those people, Pitchpenny? I'll bet you haven't. They walk around like zombies."

After the conversation with Smoking Snake, Mané Pitchpenny couldn't stop thinking about the matter.

He too had noticed something strange in the air, but the commotion those days left no time to reflect on what was happening. The bar was always packed, and consumption ran high of rum and appetizers–fried sardines, breaded meatballs, and turnovers, which his wife Celestial Archangel prepared first thing every morning. It's true that the strangers came into the bar and ordered things, but now he recalled that they never spoke; they merely pointed a finger at what they wanted, paid, and he took their money, gave them their change and took care of the next customer. They simply didn't speak. With anyone. The older customers chatted loudly, made jokes, teased one another, played cards, and ignored the "living dead." Mané Pitchpenny was getting so uneasy that he decided to speak with his wife Archangel that very night about the conversation he'd had with Smoking Snake.

Celestial Archangel, an irascible woman from Paraíba, well known around town for her ignorance and her thundering voice spewing out profanities, answered her husband's commentaries with vitriolic insults:

"I don't understand why an old sonofabitch like you should listen to a piece of shit like Smoking Snake."

More than disappointed, Pitchpenny was humiliated at his wife's reaction and decided to have a talk with Neco Silvino. The fisherman said that he not only understood but shared his friend's doubts and fears.

Together they decided to consult Hortênsia Flores on a Monday, All Souls Day. But the medium was overwhelmed by so many spirits at once that the message from beyond came through garbled. Finally, one Tobias, from Arsenal Maior, "descended" and said, "The avengers are going to take back all that was stolen from them. The time has come to settle accounts. No stone will be left standing in the fortress."

Back from her trance, Hortênsia Flores remembered nothing. In vain the two friends tried to obtain a more concrete, "down-to-earth" explanation. The clairvoyant merely smiled and said that she was only a vessel for the spirit to manifest itself and had no power to decipher what came through her.

"Good night. Go in peace, brothers." She said goodbye to them at the garden gate, which was covered with mignonettes whose sweetish perfume lingered in their nostrils for the rest of the week.

AND THE MEN, the women, the children, wagons, mules, barrows continued to come, more and more, and still more. They seemed to multiply daily. My mother became alarmed at the invasion because it was no longer only a matter of the Mangueiral. The strangers were invading our neighborhood, our streets, and even our houses. Many of them came barging in unceremoniously to drink water on our porch, without even asking permission.

"They're insolent. And weird. They've turned the estate upside down. They've dug up the Vergares' land a fistful at a time. I don't know what they want. There's nothing left to look for there," my mother said anxiously.

"Then why don't they give up?" Maria Belarmina asked.

"Because of the house, people. They've got their eye on it," answered my grandfather Zé Garbas.

"That's true," Felícia agreed. "Till now nobody had the courage to touch the house."

The huge old Vergare house continued intact, larger than ever now that there were no more trees, walls, or fences blocking the view. The rust color had been transformed into dark gray, and the gates and tiles reflected the same shade. It stood there, imposing, in the center of the terrain like a feudal castle affirming the lord's power over his dominions. The strangers would look at it from afar. At other times they would approach. They circled it. Withdrew. A movement that repeated itself daily like a war dance.

The house took on a personality and became the focus of discussion in Pedra Canga. According to many, it had moods–varying from total happiness to the deepest depression, from love to boundless hate–that manifested themselves by change in color.

"Listen here, Neco Silvino, you're full of it. Who ever heard of a house changing color on its own?" said Mané Pitchpenny, irritated.

Neco Silvino insisted it was true and that he had observed that sometimes, early in the morning, it was white and luminous and at other times red, spewing fire as if it were vomiting hatred. That's what it was: The house spoke and showed its feeling by its colors.

"Good heavens, the incredible stories it could tell...." said Pulquéria, the dreamer.

Luíza Branquinha thought it was just something people had made up, since the house was the same as it ever was; it hadn't changed color at all, and besides that, "a house is a house, and people are people, for heaven's sake."

Marcola didn't share her opinion. There was something to the whole thing. The house had held so many secrets, so many passions, so many strong emotions, that it was quite possible that those energies had remained impregnated in the walls and at certain moments took over the house, or rather "used the house as a vehicle to manifest themselves to people."

I asked Marcola if she'd seen any manifestation of the house and she said yes. So often that she was used to it. I insisted she tell me at least one of her experiences and she said that the most upsetting had been on the day she saw the house blue all over and soft music seemed to rise from the depths of the earth. She stopped to listen and clearly distinguished a woman's voice singing a sweet lullaby. She said she didn't remember the exact words but knew that the song spoke of the sadness of a mother who died and left her newborn son, without being able to care for him and watch him grow. Listening to Marcola, I felt such powerful emotion that I didn't even realize she had begun to sing. A soft voice coming from the heart of a young mother enveloped my body and I allowed myself to be rocked to it:

> Sleep, my child, sleep in peace
> Your mother's here to protect you
> I left this world all too soon

But I never meant to neglect you
For all your life I'll always be
Your constant morning star
The sun, the moonbeam that you see
To light your pathway from afar
The gentle wind above you
To guide you and to love you
Sleep, my child
Sleep, Nastácio, sleep

Marcola fell silent, touched me lightly and asked me to excuse her for going so long without saying anything; it was because she was trying to recall the song.

"But that's how it is, my dear, when you're getting on and your memory's not what it used to be," she said as she headed off slowly toward the Coxipó river.

Felícia hadn't been seen much lately, kept busy with births in Conceição das Almas, a small neighboring town of about 1200 inhabitants. When she finally returned to Pedra Canga, I found her at Rachid's general store on a rather hot afternoon in mid-August when the earth itself seemed about to catch on fire. We talked for a long time. Felícia was a calm sort of person, never in a hurry, who liked to talk but was also an excellent listener. The topic came around to the Vergare house and she told me what she had seen "on a moonlit night, as clear as day." As usual, she was returning from

Maria Belarmina's house, after dinner, with a bundle of clothes to starch–an extra task she took on to help with expenses, since she made very little as a midwife.

"Not to mention that most times they pay me in chickens, pigs, and produce," she said, smiling. "Anyway," she continued, in her soft way of speaking, "I was still a long way from the house when I saw a bright light, brighter than the moon. I was a little scared, why lie? But I decided to see up close what it was."

Everyone knew that Felícia was a brave person, honest, always faithful to the truth, never exaggerating or twisting the facts.

"When I got closer, I saw that the entire house looked like a brilliant crystal, shining like a diamond. It was so white, so very white, so full of light that I was nearly blinded. I heard music being played on a church organ, and little by little I recognized it. It was the Ave Maria, beyond a doubt. Then a nice-looking young man all in white crossed the patio going toward the house and I recognized Antônio dos Anjos, dressed just like he was when he married Maria dos Anjos. I smelled the pleasant scent of orange blossoms.... I got emotional. I always get emotional at weddings."

I asked how long she had watched the scene. She said she didn't remember; it could have been as little as a second or as long as an eternity. She only knew that when she left, she looked back and saw nothing.

The house was there, gloomy and sad as always. And dawn was breaking.

I spoke with Maria Belarmina and she told me she'd never seen any difference in the house but believed it could have happened and that it was a fact that only some people had the power of seeing the phenomenon, like Marcola and Felícia, for example. I mentioned Neco Silvino's name to complete the list, and she replied, "Forget it. He didn't see a thing. He just likes to hear himself talk."

The house manifested itself to my grandfather as he was returning late one night from a party at the home of his friend Serafim Querêncio. Taking a short-cut, he passed in front of the house, carrying his in-separable guitar and dragging his worn sandals, specially manufactured by his nephew Emiliano Gutierrez. He was walking slowly, thinking of the excuse he would make up this time for Granny Donana for getting in so late, when suddenly he looked at the house and shuddered. It was as green as an emerald and shone so brightly that "it hurt my eyes." My grandfather said he was "flabbergasted" but felt no fear. Just the opposite. He experienced a feeling of happiness, felt young, in his prime once again. And in love. As he told it, the vision of the house was dazzling and there was the perfume of bridal bouquet in the evening air.

"It was beautiful. It looked like a vain young girl all

dressed up for a dance and on the way to meet her true love," Grandfather concluded, a dreamy look in his eyes. A look that retreated before his companions at the Gimme More.

"That guitar player can really tell some big ones," grumbled Mané Pitchpenny.

Ludovica Hosteater called on the people to pray. Satan was loose. Terrible things could happen. Maybe this was the Sign. Intrigued, Pulquéria asked Ludovica if the town council had decided to put up stop signs in Pedra Canga.

"It'll be great. Lots of cars, lots of bicycles, lots of good-looking men. Civilization and progress are coming to our area."

Ludovica indignantly replied that it was because of things like this that the people were suffering. Ignorance of Holy Scripture was a proven fact. If no one knew what the Sign was, it was because no one had read the Good Book. And she decided to launch a manifesto in which she called upon the community to gather beneath the Royal Fig Tree to pray. She also took advantage of the opportunity to clarify the meaning of the Sign.

Hosteater eagerly explained that, according to Holy Scripture, God would send a SIGN to warn his people that the end of the world was coming so that all could prepare for the Final Judgment and that at that Judgment the good would be placed on the right hand–Heaven–and the evil on the left hand–Hell. At that point in her manifesto, my grandfather Zé Garbas leaped up and said this wasn't religion, it was politics, and that the manifesto had been written by the military and that its intent was clear: "sticking it to the Left" by condemning that side to hell.

Ludovica was furious and said my grandfather was an inveterate sinner and a rumpot who had no respect for sacred things: "To think that this black sheep had the nerve to steal Father Guilhermino's wine, which is reserved for Holy Mass."

Grandfather paid not the slightest heed to Hosteater's words and said that a priest should drink water and leave the alcohol to sinners like him.

ZIGMUNDO and his group were a bit bored. The journeys to and from the Mangueiral no longer held any risk. Nor could they be called a dangerous adventure. They had become routine.

"What about the house?" Chico asked. "I think we oughta try and get inside."

"I don't know," Ângelo answered. "We gotta think long and hard about it 'cause something mighty funny's going on around there. Even the old folks don't have the nerve to take a chance. We better forget it."

Ângelo's advice was not only ignored; it also served to awaken the group's spirit of adventure. That was just what they needed—a challenge. And this time a great deal of courage was necessary.

"All who wanna go, raise their hands. All who don't are out of the group on account of being a coward," proposed Zigmundo, the leader.

Ângelo tried to protest, saying that was an undemocratic way of bringing a motion for a vote, but he was cut off by Helmet Head, who said he was sure of the legality of the act because he'd heard his father say that was how politicians made decisions in the military government. No further objection was raised. They scheduled the housebreaking for that same afternoon.

With Zigmundo in the lead, followed by the others, they set off for the Mangueiral estate. They began at the back door, whose rather rusty locks might offer little resistance. They took an assortment of tools ranging from hammer to crowbar. They tried unsuccessfully for over two hours. Finally, exhausted, they stopped to discuss the matter. Maybe someone had a better idea. The windows might be the answer, but they were very high and the boys had no ladder, ropes, or other equipment. João Gonçalo was the first to hear noises and voices coming from inside the house, then Miguelito, Evilázio, and finally Chico, who leapt up and shouted, "Let's get out of here, guys! There's people in the house." No one waited to be asked twice.

The boys spread the news of what had happened. Incredulity and amazement could be seen in many a face. It was a new development, one that shook Pedra Canga. So the house wasn't empty?

Pulquéria said she didn't believe the boys. It wasn't possible for normal people to live so long in a sealed house without seeing the light of day. She herself had never been able to spend an entire day in the house. Neco Silvino was of the opinion that the residents weren't people but spirits that would never leave. Mané Pitchpenny said he didn't believe it, that such a story could only be "the fabrication of kids with nothing to do."

Commentaries proliferated. Contradictory hunches. Arguments. Tempers flared. It was in this climate that the idea arose of forming the Gutsy Group—both men and women were welcome—whose main purpose was to "put an end once and for all to such doubts, with an eye above all to social well-being, as the mysteries of the house were beginning to interfere with the town's daily life and occasioning a disturbance in the bosom of respectable families," to quote the words of Honorata Fizzwater, who taught Morals and Civics at Heart of Jesus High School.

An incipient irritation was taking hold of people and quickly turning to rage. Who were the Vergares to dare even after death to challenge the patience of the law-abiding folk of Pedra Canga? Maria Belarmina said she thought it was an insult.

"In my humble opinion, the house is the symbol of the Vergares' arrogance and is there just to humiliate us."

Agripino Soares, the town councilman elected with the largest percentage of votes, used the house as theme for his reelection campaign, at the rally he held in the city of St. Jezebel.

"My friends, the time has come to expunge from our

history the name of despotic landowners, those monsters who while living inflicted on us the misfortune of the latifundio and who now, after death, have formed a conclave of spirits at the Mangueiral estate to terrorize the gentle people of Pedra Canga. I exhort my illustrious fellow citizens to take a stance in the face of this otherworldly affront. I compare that house to the Bastille. It is the symbol of power and oppression. We must tear it down and free ourselves forever from the memory of that dark phase of our nation's history."

Lots of people didn't exactly understand what he meant by the Bastille, and some of them confused it with Camille, owner of the local cabaret. Juvenal Mendes, Agripino's amanuensis, acted quickly to clear up the misunderstanding; a wise move. He avoided a scene, on the verge of forming on the right side of the platform, instigated by defenders of Madam Camille's right to keep her house in the city.

Perhaps the idea of forming the Crusade of the Living instead of the Gutsy Group–it seems the name offended the sensitivity of certain elements–was born at that memorable rally, or maybe between drinks at the Gimme More. What is certain is that the project gathered strength and soon numbered among its adherents some thirteen volunteers. The plan was to break down the door, open all the windows, confront the spirits face to face–if necessary–and stand watch over the house until "the triumph of Good over Evil," this latter a contribution from Ludovica Hosteater to the Crusade's bylaws.

So the Crusade of the Living set out armed with tools, rosaries, holy water, salt, rue leaves, candles, and a cross made from the purest Bahian rosewood. They worked all afternoon on the locks, hinges, and doorways until their efforts were finally rewarded. They broke down the door. They heard the sound of the door crashing thunderously onto the floor tiles, followed by a scream so piercing that it echoed throughout the house for several minutes. It seemed never to end. But the people did not retreat; they went forward. They entered the house.

My grandfather Zé Garbas later compared that act to the deflowering of a virgin and went around saying that they had finally overcome her resistance and blasted her cherry to smithereens. Protests showered down on him, with Ludovica leading the pack. My grandfather laughed like crazy, taking on any and all challenges.

"He has no sense of shame," someone said.

Several newspapers published accounts of the incident. I clipped an article from the *Journal of Commerce*, written by Barão Canabrava:

A group calling itself the Crusade of the Living, made up of thirteen people (six men and seven women), broke into the Vergare mansion yesterday on the Mangueiral estate. They were determined to carry out what they felt to be a sacred mission: to take the last stronghold of the enemy who for many years enslaved, killed, and robbed hundreds of innocent people. The family's tyranny caused poverty and suffering. The untouched house–erect, haughty, rising in the center of the estate–was the symbol of the Vergares' domination. Though dead or disappeared, their presence would continue as long as the house remained inviolate. No one could feel free of the oppression of the past. It was necessary to overcome the longstanding fear transmitted from generation to generation among the residents of Pedra Canga. Thus the invasion of the Mangueiral mansion, in the view of the noted historian Carvalho Furtado, "was not an act of vandalism but the conscious taking of a position by the oppressed against the oppressor." As proof of his statement the scholar points to the fact that to the present moment no object of value has been taken from inside the mansion, which continues luxurious, magnificent, and splendid in its furnishings, chandeliers, and silverware. It appears that the actions of the "Crusade of the Living" did not spring from any material motive.

Perhaps because of the newspaper reports or the comments of those who had been inside the mansion, others, attracted by the scent of novelty, began to appear from all sides. They were few at first and came timidly, skittishly, circling the house for a time before going in. As the hours passed, more appeared. The in-and-out pace accelerated incredibly. They began picking up small objects: candleholders, porcelain knick-knacks, vases, plates, cutlery. Then the tablecloths and bed linens, and the family's clothing–some of it so old and yellowed by time that it wasn't worth hauling away. But they didn't care. They took everything. As in the beginning, they brought sacks, handcarts, wagons, donkeys. The bundles grew. Entire families, including small children, came more than twice a day and left straining under their burdens.

I saw they were the same unfamiliar types as before. Pale and mute, they worked rapidly like someone obeying a schedule. The anthill had begun to function again. Except this time its hunger was voracious. Nothing would prevent its devouring everything in its path.

"theft" into a "loan," my conscience calmed in the face of the new terminology that camouflaged my act. I went home at peace, with the intention of beginning the reading that very night.

Beginning? But who said I could stop? I read the diary from cover to cover. When I finished, I heard a rooster crow, not three times as in the New Testament when Christ told the apostle Peter: "Peter, this night, before the cock crows thrice, thou shalt betray me." The cock crowed only once, enough to remind me that the reading was over, that my head was spinning, and that I must betray the authors of the diary, by publishing the secret ceremonies recorded in it.

I didn't know where to start. I was upset by the discovery and frightened by its content. I had never heard of so much evil in one place, practiced by an entire family against human beings and animals. And what repelled me most was that they described the scenes as naturally as if they were speaking of fulfilling a duty. In some passages they clearly expressed their pleasure at their practices. I don't know if they were unaware, perverse, insane, fanatics, or what. It was difficult to categorize them. Maybe, by themselves, they formed a new classification of human beings born with some mental or spiritual aberration. Was it possible?

I couldn't conceive of the Vergares practicing such crimes for years on end and never being punished. At least no one had heard of a Vergare ever being arrested or indicted for a crime. They had lived their entire lives with impunity. There's a popular saying: "Whatever we do on earth, we pay for it here and now." But that didn't hold for the Vergares. According to Hortênsia Flores, the seer, they would pay for it all in the other world.

"They're going to burn in hellfire forever."

But I had my doubts even about that. With so many diabolical rituals and such an intimate relationship with Satan, who knows? Hell might be a paradise for them.

Marcola got very angry when I expressed these thoughts. She said I didn't understand a thing about other realities, had no faith, and certainly had never read *The Book of Spirits*, where the law of cause and effect was quite clear. Very surprised at her reaction, I asked if she had read that book and she replied, "I haven't actually read it, but I've heard about it, and I know that Cause and Effect at the spiritual level means that whatever you do, you receive it in turn, so if you do Evil, you get Evil in return. Understand?"

I did understand of course, but I still didn't understand Marcola, a simple woman of the people who sometimes showed herself to have deep knowledge of certain matters and to be well equipped with every argument to defend her point of view.

The diary was a document that proved many of the

stories recounted by the people. In the prevailing view, the Vergares had a pact with the devil. From the description of the ceremonies I concluded that they took place at a special site inside the house. But where? I decided to return there to investigate. Plantation owners usually had their own chapel at home, where they met to pray or attended Mass, weddings, or baptisms when some priest visited the plantation. People said that the Vergares had one, but I couldn't reconcile the data in my head about the ritual site with the limited space of a chapel. Something didn't fit.

I went through the entire house without finding what I was looking for. I went upstairs, rummaged through everything, returned to the ground floor, went through every room. Nothing. I sat on the floor in one completely empty drawing room and reflected that maybe I had been mistaken and there was no special site. Tired, I lay down on the floor, trying to relax and coordinate my thoughts, when I heard a sound beneath my head like a rat gnawing wood. I rose, startled, looked around and saw that I had lain down on top of a trapdoor. How could I have forgotten? Of course the house–like all of its type–must have a cellar. I lifted the trapdoor hatch and discovered some steps. I tried to go down but there was total darkness and I couldn't see a thing. I gave up. I replaced the hatch and decided to return later with a flashlight.

I remember that the afternoon I decided to go back to the house I saw on my dressing table the gold crucifix and chain that my grandmother Donana had given me and which I'd never worn. To be on the safe side, I put it around my neck and left in search of the place I judged to be the center of resistance of the powerful family.

I THOUGHT IT very strange when that morning I found a letter from Ludovica among my correspondence. A pink envelope with a green olive branch printed in the left-hand corner. Curious, I quickly opened it, not having the faintest idea of its contents. In a delicate, carefully sculpted hand, this was Hosteater's letter in its entirety:

Dear Madam,

As fate would have it, a page of your future "almanac" has fallen into my hands, in which you are cavalier enough to cite the New Testament in transcribing passages from Holy Gospel that never existed.

In good conscience I, Ludovica Trindade do Cravo, can only consider it bad faith on your part, for I cannot believe that you are sufficiently unfamiliar with the Good Book that you would commit so many errors, culminating in a total distortion of the facts.

Thus, motivated by the most righteous indignation, I am writing to correct the errors contained in this passage, before it is too late. In the first place, the one who betrayed our Lord Jesus Christ was not Peter but JUDAS. As for the rooster, it only crowed *once*, and the true words of our betrayed Lord Jesus Christ were as follows: "Peter, this night, before the cock crow, thou shalt *deny* me thrice."

With the tranquillity of having fulfilled my duty as a good Christian, I close with the reminder that next time, if you wish to cite Holy Scripture, do so correctly, consulting books or other sources authorized by the Holy Mother Church.

(s) Ludovica Trindade do Cravo
President of the Sisterhood of the Daughters of Mary

I didn't understand how Ludovica could have read my manuscripts or even gotten her hands on them. I ran to my room and saw to my horror that the notebook where I wrote this narrative was open to exactly the page she had cited. I asked my mother if Ludovica had been in the house and she confirmed that she had. On the pretext of buying a pullet to make chicken soup, Ludovica had my mother go to the backyard where the coop was and take a great deal of time there till she found a "feathered friend" that met Hosteater's demands: "pretty, nice and yellow with brown spots, not too fat and not too thin, and above all a virgin, good-natured and happy."

My mother did the impossible to satisfy Ludovica but in the end the hypocrite looked at the chosen pullet with displeasure and said she didn't like the chicken's face.

"And she left without so much as a thank you for the work I did," my mother complained.

I asked what had happened and she said the only thing strange that she'd noticed was that when she went to the backyard Ludovica was sitting in the living room and when she returned she saw Ludovica hastily leaving my room "like somebody who's got something to hide."

It wasn't hard to guess the rest. Hosteater had of course come to my house for the sole purpose of snooping into my writings.

What about the diary? Had she read or leafed through the greenish-gray book, even briefly? I concluded she hadn't, as she made no mention of it in the letter. Knowing Ludovica the way I did, I knew she would never refrain from menacing me with hellfire because, at the very least, I was living in mortal sin by the mere fact of having such a cursed book in my possession.

Since nothing was missing, I decided to forget the incident, and I kept the Green Book in my custody. But things didn't end there.

My mother mentioned the subject to my grandfather Zé Garbas and bang! That was all it took. The egg hit the fan. My grandfather said who was Ludovica to give me lessons about Holy Scripture, and that the Book could be interpreted a thousand ways, and furthermore, what did it matter if it was St. Peter or Judas who betrayed Jesus? For him, denying or handing the Man over to the men was the same kind of betrayal and they were both disciples and therefore "two peas in a pod." He not only told all and sundry about the matter, he also–and this is the worst part–decided to get satisfaction from Ludovica right at the door of St. Gonçalo's on a Sunday after nine o'clock Mass. The courtyard was packed with people when my grandfather, guitar in hand and drunk as a skunk, challenged Ludovica to a song-duel. Just imagine the scene. Ludovica pretended not to notice, but that attitude didn't last long. Grandfather bellowed that he was talking to her and asked if, besides being a priest's mistress she was deaf to boot. After that, Ludovica had no choice but to accept the challenge. To her regret! My grandfather was prepared with a verse on the tip of his tongue. He picked up his guitar, and his elephant's lungs loosed upon the air the "Song of the True Truth":

Hosteater, leave my granddaughter alone
Mind your own business, you nosy old crone
Don't try to fool us–a virgin you're not
We're all aware who got into your twat
Manuelão proved that he's no fairy
He's the one who got your cherry
Don't try to let on it's such a big shock
When he's known by all for his twelve-inch cock.

It was too much. Ludovica fainted and was succored by the Daughters of Mary, who carried her bodily into the church. The crowd was divided; many laughed uproariously, some censured grandfather's lack of respect, while others wandered away commenting that "Old Sulfurmouth" was really vomiting fire today and that anyone with a "tail of straw" should tuck it in and head straight home. The guitarist had outdone himself. And for several days not even my grandmother Donana would speak to him.

I ARRIVED at the Mangueiral at nightfall and went straight to the trapdoor. I tried to open it but couldn't. It appeared to be locked from inside. But how could that be? I was sure it had been open earlier, and I hadn't seen a lock or latch. After several attempts I concluded I needed help.

I went to the Gimme More and found Big Tomás. I asked him to help me and when I explained the details of the task I sensed his apprehension, but he said he'd go, on one condition: "I can break open the trapdoor, but from there on it's up to you. I don't want to get involved in things from the other world."

I accepted. We went to the Mangueiral and Big Tomás opened the trapdoor without difficulty, as it wasn't locked. I had no explanation for my friend. What can you say at a time like that? I swore that the trapdoor had been locked; otherwise I wouldn't have called on him, but Big Tomás gave me a very suspicious look as if to say, "Hey, I know you said that just to have someone along with you."

Not wanting an argument, I said that on second thought I must have been mistaken. Big Tomás replied that it was nothing, said goodbye–"May your Guardian Angel protect you, sister"–and ran out the door.

I can't deny that I felt nervous upon seeing myself alone. My first inclination was to leave. Maybe some other day, I thought. But deep down I knew the time was now. There was no room for delay.

Turning on the flashlight, I descended the narrow steps and began to inspect the place. It was an immense room with damp stone walls that smelled of mold. Rats, bats, and cockroaches roamed at will. There was no furniture. In the middle was an enormous slab, thick and rectangular. On the floor, various objects: an ax, a large knife, a hammer, nails, an old trunk, masks, coils of rope. Examining them up close, I remembered with horror the ceremonies described in the diary and, perhaps from being in the place where they had been held, I visualized the restoration of the past in all its force. I sensed the presence of people gathering to prepare the ritual, chants, shouts, and a constant murmur that seemed to come from the depths of the earth.

Terrified, I saw rise from the back of the room a shape in a red tunic that came slowly toward me, holding a large razor-sharp dagger. It looked like a peccary, but its head was human. It guffawed, howled, and bellowed: water, water, water. I tried to flee, but my feet seemed nailed to the ground and I had no control over the rest of my body. I heard a buzzing in my ears and suddenly felt so weak that I nearly fainted. Then I heard noises on the steps. I focused the light in that direction and saw Marcola, radiant and dressed in white, with necklaces of the god Oxóssi around her throat. In a firm voice she ordered me to get up and follow her at once.

To this day I don't know how I managed to carry out her order to the letter. I leaped up as if a bolt of electricity had entered me and went with her. Together we left the house. On the way home I was puzzled by the rapidity and confidence of Marcola's pace. To tell the truth, I had to make an effort to keep up with her. I asked why she was in such a hurry but she didn't answer. Nor did she look at me. She quickened her step. Almost running, I fell further and further behind, the distance between Marcola and me increasing more and more until she turned the corner of Serenity street and disappeared from my sight. When I reached that point I couldn't see her anymore and didn't understand where she could have gone. The street was deserted and all the houses were shut because of the lateness of the hour.

I was still trembling when I got home. Since the light was on in my mother's bedroom, I went to see if she needed anything. I found her sitting in a rocking chair beside the bed, where Marcola lay in a deep sleep. Not understanding just what I was seeing, I asked her what was going on. She told me that Marcola had arrived at nightfall complaining of a strong headache and fever.

She told Marcola to get in bed, gave her a hot lemon verbena tea and an aspirin, and covered her with two wool blankets so she could sweat the sickness from her body. It was an old custom practiced by virtually the entire population of Pedra Canga. Before calling Tadeu the pharmacist to diagnose whatever illness came along–from whitlow to mumps or chickenpox–any mother would apply a good "sweating" to the sick person to see how he reacted. If the results were negative, the thing to do was resort to medicine from the pharmacy. Tadeu, who was intimately familiar with the local illnesses, cheerfully attended one and all. They said he had even cured venereal disease. And with total discretion.

My mother wouldn't stop talking about Marcola, saying she had fallen asleep quivering and twitching and was even delirious, uttering lots of disconnected phrases and repeating over and over: "They're going to cut off her head, they're going to cut off her head." But my mother hadn't worried, because delirium was quite common in cases of high fever. I asked if Marcola had left the house in the last few hours and she thought the question was odd. She replied rather curtly, asking if I was all right in the head and if I was seeing straight. How could a person in Marcola's condition get up and go walking around at night? She also said she "hadn't slept a wink," remaining at her friend's side the entire time, and could guarantee that at no moment had Marcola set foot outside.

I went to my room with my head pounding. So much had happened, and I could find no rational explanation for the sequence of events. I remembered Marcola once calling my attention to the side of me that thirsted for concrete answers to things that happen beyond the bounds of the testimony of our senses.

I sat in a chair, looking about me for something I couldn't specify, when I saw the empty place. What place? The place where I kept the diary. I began to search the entire room, in the most unlikely spots: under the bed, behind the door, in a flower vase, inside the chamber pot. Nothing. It had disappeared. The only thing I found was a large green grasshopper, of the kind people call a praying mantis because it always holds its hands as if it were in prayer. I asked it to leave or at least to give me a clue as to where the greenish-gray book had gone, but apparently it was in no mood to talk or get involved in the mysterious disappearance. It took flight in the direction of the yard. Automatically, I followed. After that I don't know what became of it. To tell the truth, I forgot the praying mantis. I lost interest in its fate. Could it have been the bearer of some message I was unable to decipher?

I lay down under the guava tree where I used to play with my dog Fido when I was a child. I wanted to find myself again but didn't know how. I tried to concentrate on the recent happenings but my head opened so much space for Fido that he appeared, leaping merrily, wagging his tail ceaselessly. Together we relived a thousand playful moments. We ran from the yard and played hide-and-seek until I grew tired and lay down, my face resting on the ground, my body next to Fido's. He told me this was the best position for regaining the energy lost in the "counterbalance of time" and for rediscovering the rhythm of my heart that had been disordered by the "men in skirts."

When I awoke, dawn was breaking and the rising sun was promising a lot of heat ahead.

I went back to my room with the idea firmly in mind of writing down what I had experienced in the last few hours, but first I went through the kitchen and found my mother and Marcola drinking tea and chatting away. They didn't even see me as I passed. Life in Pedra Canga was being discussed there in our kitchen with customary fervor.

I fled to avoid getting drawn in. I wanted to deal with words–a vital form that doesn't let memories die. And my sister Glória years later would confirm that, though a baby in our mother's arms at the time, she noticed the rapidity of my steps and the look of determination on my face, like someone seeking her mother's breast for the first feeding of the day.

And the living dead continued their pilgrimage. Day and night. Night and day. Through rain, sun, and mist. Through skies starry, dark, or cloudy. Through wind, heat, or bitter cold. They ignored it all. The anthill boiled. What force drove those people to move, move, move, carry, carry, carry? Who were they and where had they come from? Jovina Parisienne, the most recent acquisition at the Open Heaven, confided to Big Tomás, her intimate friend, that she'd tried to "hook" one of those "strollers" but hadn't succeeded. She said she was received with a cold stare, one of pure disdain, and a phrase of which she hadn't understood a word: "I'm not interested in fresh meat." What did that mean? Big Tomás said he didn't know either, but if she wanted some advice, the best thing she could do was stay away from those people. Parisienne was never again seen in the area of hot nighttime merrymaking.

Finally, the "pilgrims" emptied the house. When I saw them pass with pile after pile of books I thought that the raid had come to an end. Far from it. It was merely the beginning of a new phase. They returned armed with tools of every sort, which they used to yank out windows, doors, portals, window sashes, skylights, tiles, ceiling adornments, iron bars, and everything else. And the cargo processions continued.

"They're like rats. They're going to gnaw away at the house till nothing's left but the bones," said Luíza Branquinha.

"What's that got to do with us? As long as they don't come sniffing around our houses…" said Felícia, concerned.

Maria Belarmina, very sure of herself, tried to calm her friend: "You can rest easy. If your conscience is clear you have nothing to worry about. That rabble is just going to attack the Mangueiral. It's punishment. Divine justice may be slow but it always comes."

Smoking Snake hurled countless imprecations against those he called "usurpers," but between one drink of rum and the next he contradicted himself completely by stating that it was exactly that, the punishment of the Vergares, the true usurpers of the Mangueiral. He cited the name of my grandfather Zé Garbas, saying that the singing guitarist knew the whole story. When my grandfather was "in high spirits" he would hug Smoking Snake and sing the old melody about Maria dos Anjos, but sometimes he'd tell Smoking Snake to go soak his head, because he had no truck with dissolute winos who weren't above stealing rum from the voodoo offerings left at crossroads for the native saints. Smoking Snake retorted that he didn't see any difference between voodoo rum and church wine, and everybody knew of my grandfather's nocturnal visits to the sacristy at St. Gonçalo's.

The one who became furious at these disputes was my grandmother Donana, who could never resign herself to my grandfather's predilection for "rabble"–the word she used for common people who weren't "from good families," or rather, who didn't belong to a certain social class, the so-called "best" class, so to speak.

"I don't know who he took after. You'd never know he was descended from nobility."

According to her, my great-grandfather don Garanhon y Garbas Gutierrez was a Spanish nobleman whose ancestors had been part of the Court. The teachings that he transmitted to his children could be termed unequaled, in all senses.

"As proof, a book entitled *Rules for Good Living* was read every evening at the table, before dinner."

I asked for further information about the book and Granny, very pleased at my interest, continued, "Basically the book was a study of good manners. It contained rules like how a gentleman should act in the most diverse circumstances in society. The man had the finest upbringing. A nobleman!"

Grandfather's behavior, exactly the opposite of his forebear, was a mystery to her. Every time she tried to talk sense to him–when he was sober–he would listen in silence, appearing to agree with everything she said, but that didn't last long. The first time he got drunk he'd come home insulting my grandmother, calling her a liar, saying that she was getting senile and had always had delusions of grandeur and that as far as he knew he never had an ancestor who was a count or a duke, whatever the hell it was, and that the only thing he knew for sure was his father used to dress as a marquise for Carnival and parade with the Royal Stags, ready for anything and everything, drunk as a lord and looking for trouble.

When the level descended to this point, my grandmother, already ashamed at what the neighbors would think, would withdraw to her room, take up her rosary, and begin a novena to St. Rita of Lost Causes.

Looking back, I can see that she truly believed that one day her patron saint would listen to her. The redemption of my grandfather came to be her reason for living, once the children were grown and married and had provided a passel of noisy grandchildren to shatter the tranquillity of the house.

I MADE A DECISION. I would bring everything out in the open with Marcola. I hadn't been dreaming, and I wasn't drunk. Everything had happened just as it happened. Marcola appeared at the house at the exact moment to save me from some terrible thing that I could not name. From death, certainly. But in what way would they have killed me? And does it matter? Strangulation or beheading, the result would be the same–I would be dead and buried by now without even having time to make the sign of the Cross.

I arrived at Marcola's house in late afternoon. The sky was dark and a strong wind was blowing, preparing for rain. She wasn't there, but I decided to wait. I couldn't take anymore the uncertainty buzzing through my head. My mother had told me that Marcola hadn't left our house that night. I had to believe her; she was horrified by lies. She used to say that death itself wouldn't make her tell even one lie. And Marcola was also a truthful woman. The truth had to come out. How? By speaking to Marcola herself, of course. Why hadn't I thought of it before? The key to the mystery could only be in the hands of that powerful woman for whom, it seemed, heaven and earth coexisted in a single dimension.

As I waited for Marcola I tried to control myself and told my heart not to beat so fast because the answers I sought would soon be given to me. In reality, I wanted Marcola to confirm what had happened, because I refused to admit that my eyes had sent my brain images that didn't correspond to the reality of that night. And what about my body? I still trembled and felt chills up my spine when I recalled it... How could it *not* have happened? Impossible! Marcola would put an end to this anguish that had become part of my life and prodded at my soul, shaking my conception of things, stealing my sleep, pushing me from my dreams.

Around five o'clock Marcola showed up, her steps dragging, a pot of water on her head. As soon as she saw me, she smiled broadly: "What're you doing here, missy? You didn't come here just to see me. I see a green ring of anxiety 'round your head. You need to talk to me, don't you?"

A bit embarrassed, I stammered a few disjointed excuses but soon stopped, dominated by Marcola's gaze, which was scrutinizing my soul. I said yes, I needed to talk to her about a matter that was consuming me.

Marcola squatted in the doorway, filled her pipe and lighted it, took a puff, and said, "Let's parley, missy.

You're very upset. You need to put an end to the doubts growing around your chest like a vine and suffocating you. Say everything you feel."

I didn't hesitate for a second. Words crashing against one another, almost without breathing I spit out the events of that night, beginning with my arriving at the cellar of the Vergare house. Marcola listened calmly, without interrupting, without looking at me, as if she weren't even there. I had the impression that only her body was still before me; her soul had flown to someplace that she alone knew. All I could do was wait till she returned. But as soon as I finished, she pierced me with a glance deep inside me and said:

"Missy is mistaken. The Vergare house doesn't have, and never has had, a cellar."

In desperation I almost invoked Big Tomás's name as witness, but then I remembered that he hadn't gone with me down the ladder leading to the cellar. He had merely seen the entrance, which by all indications must have been a trapdoor. That was surely what my friend would say if he were asked.

I argued with Marcola. I said she couldn't deny she was there, since I had seen her clearly in the flash of light. Her gaze once more in the distance, staring at the world's immensity, she replied, "Your steps took you where you wanted to go. Your eyes showed you what you wanted to see. Your flashlight caught the form of the one you wanted close to you. But your soul wasn't there. Things didn't happen on the plane on which you persist in basing your truth. More than once I've told you that eyes are misinformed and the mind deceives itself when it has as its only objective finding a material explanation for things that happen in other realities. There are some who succeed in navigating in the appearance of both worlds. There are others who are *here* and *there*. They lose themselves, they explode, they sunder. They confuse everything and don't know which ground to walk on. It takes a long time for the eyes to see clearly and free themselves of preconceptions. But there is a river of crystalline water running between the two sides. One need only follow its flow. The voyage is sweet because the prison doors open, boundaries fall, the body takes flight, the soul walks unshod through meadows. The spirit has flesh and the flesh possesses a spirit. The two sides are no longer; all is one."

Marcola fell into a long silence. She picked up her pipe, relighted it, took another puff, and told me that it was getting late and didn't I want to stay for dinner? She was going to fix a jerked beef stew with okra that was delicious.

I didn't know what to say. My head was spinning, and the phrase came out curtly, unbidden: "But you saved my life. You can't deny that. I feel I owe you a debt."

"If your salvation came through me, then praise be to Manu, my master."

And that ended the subject. She said she'd forgotten that I wasn't fond of gherkins but no matter. Next time I came she'd make jerked beef with squash and kale, one of my favorite dishes since childhood. She sent regards to my mother and disappeared inside her shack.

I went home reflecting on Marcola's words and felt an immense peace as if I had begun to understand their meaning. Marcola's power was so present, so real, that I felt something inside transforming itself each time I spoke with her. I was learning so much with Marcola that at times I felt physical pain at the contact with such knowledge. I told her this on one occasion and she said, "Don't be afraid, missy. The road to knowledge can be painful. But it's nothing like physical pain. Pay attention to what I'm telling you and prepare your feet for the journey."

AND THE LIVING DEAD ceased their pilgrimage. Overnight, everyone vanished. Our street went back to sleep. Silence reigned and not a single lost soul could be seen wandering about. Deserted. No one found anything strange in the disappearance of the pilgrim-plunderers. Of course not: The sack had come to an end. Only the skeleton of the house remained. The stone walls, over a yard thick, resisted the few attacks made upon them. After all, what good were the stones? Not to mention their weight. Even an experienced pack mule would have let out tremendous brays of protest if forced to haul them. The only thing left of the old Vergare property was its remains: an immense plot full of holes that bore the weight of the ruins of the old house, the erstwhile symbol of the family's power. Disregard began to infiltrate people's minds, and their eyes showed near indifference, were it not for the uncomfortable presence of the sentinel-like walls in a state of alert.

The empty plot came to have its uses: a soccer field, a trail between Pedra Canga and the Saranzal river, a place to keep wagons and oxcarts, a shortcut to the

Gimme More. Other than that, it was nothing but an immense wilderness, vanishing, losing its grandeur.

But even in their agony the Vergare dominions stubbornly exerted their presence among the people of Pedra Canga. Much was still to happen. In fact, Pulquéria went around saying a calm like that was concealing something. Maria Belarmina told her to shut up: "Why do you always have to see bad signs in everything? Whatever had to happen has happened. Now we can live in peace, thank God."

My grandfather Zé Garbas, always fond of parties, guitars, and rum, an inveterate customer of the Gimme More, usually passed by the ruins nightly on his way home. Dragging his worn sandals, the singing guitar player was essaying shopworn excuses for my grandmother. What would it be this time? Who would be to blame for his delay? Big Tomás? Neco Silvino? Maybe. Smoking Snake? Out of the question. That was the only name that infuriated the old lady, at most times self-control incarnate. In reality, no one understood why my grandfather even bothered making up stories anymore, for even Granny Donana herself had long since relieved him of the obligation to do so...

"Force of habit, friends. A habit cultivated for many years ends up owning you, it installs itself inside us and starts giving orders and we obey, thinking it's our own will doing the talking. That's a laugh," said Ezekiel the Hermit in one of his rare appearances at the Gimme More.

But I want to get back to the point where my grandfather was passing by the ruins of the large old house. First a howling wind began to blow so hard that he thought he'd be carried off or sucked into the whirlwind that had arisen and was roaring like a runaway bull. Grandfather said he clung with hands and feet to a tree and asked it not to let him be swept away; if that happened, the two of them were going together, since no power on earth would make him let go.

"I clutched at it like a drowning man," he said.

It appears that with his threat the tree put down more roots into the ground and resolved to take grandfather's side against the wind. They won. Exhausted, as if a river serpent had sucked away his strength, grandfather continued homeward. Or such was his intention. He hadn't gone two steps when he heard a woman's sobs, interspersed with wailing. He cupped his ear and sensed that the sound was coming from the ruins. He was asking himself who could be there at that hour, when he clearly heard a voice saying, "In the name of charity, bury my bones. I cannot stand to suffer such cold and humiliation. I was so beautiful in life. I had the bearing of a queen. I don't want my remains to be looked upon in horror or mockery. I want to rest in peace."

One step at a time, my grandfather entered the ruins, searching room by room, finding nothing. No one. His hair standing on end and with a creeping sensation just below his ear, he decided to get out of there. He wasn't a man to run from nothing, but just in case, what business did he have there anyway, for heaven's sake? More than once he'd dealt with things from the other world, and he knew it called for a real man. Not that he was afraid, no sir. It was just that he thought his guardian angel had already worked hard enough that night; no point in taking advantage. Face the beyond with nothing but his bare hands? Nobody was that crazy. Confronting the supernatural requires strength of knowledge and a more powerful ally at our side. He put it out of his thoughts and went straight to Granny Donana's bed. By this time she was sleeping peacefully, perhaps dreaming about dances in the royal court, gallant young men kissing her hand, fluttering fans shielding emotions, corsets imprisoning rebellious bodies. Oh, if only Zé Garbas were a nobleman, sighed my grandmother, abruptly brought back to harsh reality by the smell of rum—an aroma that she knew very well did not belong in her courtly dreams.

Grandfather had the habit of waking at daybreak. He said the sun would never find him sleeping. Unless he were dead. And that's how it happened, years later. The church clock at St. Gonçalo's struck seven a.m.

on an ordinary December day, and he continued to sleep. The others found it strange. The previous night's binge must have really been a big one. They went to take a look. Yes. He was sleeping the sleep from which he would never awaken. At that moment the singing guitarist must be making his case to St. Peter, showing off a few songs, trying to somehow win his way into heaven. I'm sure that if he didn't manage to convince the celestial gatekeeper, he found a way to enter Paradise through the back door or through a window, or maybe even by digging a hole in the walls of firmament.

Grandfather had a sleepless night. When the rooster crowed he was already up. He grated some guaraná, drank it, lit his straw cigarette, sat down in the doorway, and remained there, thinking, watching the day dawn, waiting for the first one to come along to tell of the previous night's happening. He didn't have long to wait. He saw Neco Silvino appear at the corner with his basket full of fish. From the look of things he'd had a good night fishing. Grandfather went to meet him, and, without so much as a hello, blurted out: "Know what happened to me, Neco Silvino?"

"No, but you look like somebody who's seen a ghost."

"How'd you know?"

"Just by looking at you. Ghosts leave a mark."

"What mark? Where? Listen, I don't have any kind

of mark. Stop trying to get me confused, you old liar. You always did like to make up things."

"Yeah, but now you're the one making things up. Let's have it. Get it off your chest. I'm dying to hear it."

Grandfather related in full detail passing by the house and the moans, repeating verbatim the words he'd heard. Everyone knew my grandfather had a phenomenal memory—no doubts on that score. Everyone knew grandfather wasn't afraid of anything, much less a ghost—no one cast doubts about that either. So was it true? Whose voice could it be? And whose spirit bemoaned the destruction of the house as if it were the destruction of its own body? Did the house have a spirit? The memory of the revelations about the house's feelings fitted in with this latest happening. Could the house possibly be suffering?

"How many things that house still has to say...." Pulquéria said, recalling the time of its manifestations.

Maria Belarmina said it was time to shut up about it because all they needed was for Pulquéria to start saying that everything was calm for more confusion to arise. She called Pulquéria a bird of bad omen, which was enough to set off one of their interminable shouting matches.

Comments swirled in a flurry. At the Gimme More it was the sole topic of conversation. My grandfather, more and more euphoric, added to the story with each retelling.

Opinions varied, Mané Pitchpenny, very seriously, as if testifying in a court of law, told me, "It's hard to say. My friend Zé Garbas isn't a coward; he's not afraid of ghosts and he has a fantastic memory, but he's always drunk as a skunk. Besides that, he's a storyteller with airs of being a poet. And besides, folks like that have a way of seeing reality different from other people. They live in a dream world…"

Big Tomás believed religiously in my grandfather. He was even afraid of doubting the happening: "Me? I'm not going to say I don't believe it. I could be punished and one of those things could pop up in front of me. What could I do? Good Lord. It's like I always say: You don't fool around with things from the other world."

Marcola was away for a few days in Livramento. As soon as she returned, I asked what she made of all that. She answered that she had no way of knowing if things had happened just as my grandfather had related them, then added: "The Vergare energies are still there, living at the surface of the earth, loose and uncontrolled. It's very dangerous to deal with forces that appear under deceptive forms. They try to take over the soul, dominate the mind, eat up life to resuscitate in someone else's body. There's still a lot of trial ahead, but the time of the final reckoning will arrive in the wake of the mighty star, which comes from the far reaches of St. Anthony's Hill, and guided by our Great Father."

Without really understanding Marcola's words, I ventured one more question: "But have you ever faced those forces?"

"My life has been a permanent confrontation. I've been a fighter from birth. My mother bore me standing up, at the headwaters of the world. From there I rolled down the waterfall on the current of the Xamaná river, searching for Manu, who was waiting for me at the eye of the earth."

"And the Vergares' power had no effect on you?"

"I crossed worlds on the wings of Manu, my master, who taught me how to breach the lines of the inconceivable."

I wanted to go on with the conversation, with countless questions leaping into my head, but Marcola anticipated me and said she was in a hurry and that we should leave it for another time. She walked away without looking back. I was left with the certainty that she alone could overcome the evil force that still held sway on the Mangueiral estate.

I WENT TO THE GIMME MORE to gather further information about the much-discussed "Zé Garbas vision," as the case had become known. They were already saying that grandfather planned to take advantage of the situation to launch the song of the year. As soon as I went in I could sense the excitement. Everyone was talking at once, a heavy cloud of smoke befouled the air, but Smoking Snake's voice stood out above the rest:

"Listen to what I'm telling you. Zé Garbas is exaggerating this time. I think he drank a whole barrel of Father Guilhermino's wine, and they say it's got a kick like a mule."

"What're you talking about, Smoking Snake?" I asked.

"I'll answer only because you just got here, 'cause everybody knows what I'm talking about. I'm talking about your grandfather Zé Garbas, and not behind his back either. I'll repeat every word to his face as soon as he shows up around here. I'm saying that what he heard wasn't the voice of a ghost in any way, shape, or form. Know whose voice it was? Crazy Joana, that poor soul who wanders the streets day and night looking for a place to sleep. I know her real well, and sometimes she sleeps in the cemetery. The poor woman talks, cries, moans, and tears her hair. They say she's been like that ever since her only daughter died the night before her wedding, just as she was trying on the bridal gown. Seems it was a heart attack; I'm not rightly sure. Joana went mad. Relatives took care of the girl's funeral but they didn't let her attend 'cause of her state of mind. Maybe that's why she keeps on repeating that she wants to be buried. I don't know. She's completely off her rocker. She's crazy as a bedbug."

When Smoking Snake finished talking, a short guy who'd been sitting quietly said in a loud voice, "Shut up, you voodoo whiskey thief. Don't you know Crazy Joana's been dead for ages?"

"Who told you so, Nepomuceno?"

"Nobody told me. She used to live next door to me in Hardscrabble. My wife Andiara was the one who looked after her in the last days of her illness, and she's right here to prove I'm not lying. She died with sores all over her. They told me it was an awful disease."

Smoking Snake didn't give in and continued to argue that it wasn't true and that Crazy Joana was still alive and he could prove it. Or else they weren't talking about the same Joana. A general debate ensued, with some in favor of Smoking Snake, others on

Nepomuceno's side, and a third group, pro-Zé Garbas, stating that Smoking Snake was making the whole story up just to irritate grandfather because of the old rivalry that had always existed between them.

To round out the scene, my grandfather arrived, guitar in hand and with a verse at the tip of his tongue:

> Who's Crazy Joana?
> Nobody knows her well
> It's time for Smoking Snake
> To light out straight for hell

"Bravo! Bravo!" yelled the frenetic crowd.

From outside came another shout: "The house is crying again. Come with me. The house is crying again."

In the darkness no one could clearly see who the woman was whose cries dashed cold water on the over-heated heads of the Gimme More's customers. But the answer was not long in coming. There she was, disheveled, her eyes bulging, arms spread wide, screaming her head off.

"What's going on, Pulquéria? Did you see the Evil One?" Mané Pitchpenny asked.

"Worse'n that. I saw the shape of a man, tall and wearing boots with spurs, a wide belt, and a whip in his hands, in the ruins of the Mangueiral."

"But what's so unusual about that? Maybe it's some rancher just back from Poconé. It happens all the time," Big Tomás said.

"Wait a minute. Let me finish," Pulquéria retorted. "It so happens that the man had no head. When I looked at him I felt the ground shake and heard such a soulful cry like someone who'd just lost their mother. And that wasn't all. I heard a voice say, 'Bury me deep in the ground and put an end to my suffering.' And the shape disappeared into the walls of the house."

"And then what?" Big Tomás said in a near-whisper.

Pulquéria replied that although she was shaking like a leaf, her heart was racing and she was in a cold sweat, she'd still had the courage to ask, "Who are you?"

"I am what you see. I am the house that sheltered such intense passions and can no longer bear the weight of existence. They took away my arms, my legs, my head, but my trunk still lives. They won't let me die. Why? Why?"

Pulquéria, a buzzing in her ears, didn't have the strength to go on hearing the laments that seemingly came from the walls themselves. She set out in a run and didn't stop till she reached the Gimme More, the only place in Pedra Canga open at that hour.

Neco Silvino succored his sister, attempting to calm her with a double serving of brandy. He invited her to spend the night at his house, as he saw that Pulquéria was "nervous and kind of out of it." He quickly left the bar with his sister before the others could regain their senses and deluge the poor woman with questions. What she had gone through was nothing to be taken lightly. The best thing was to go home, take a nice herb bath, pray, and hang a cross of rue branches on her bedroom door.

Pulquéria took the advice, for the first time in her life, without arguing about it. Dumfounded, caught at a weak moment, she made no objection and silently followed her brother.

Her silence lasted only as long as the walk to Neco Silvino's house, for when the latter told Maria Belarmina of the event, his wife guffawed and said, "You believe her? What nerve! She's crazy as a loon. You must be very pleased with the stir you created at the Gimme More. A glorious night for you, wasn't it, sister-in-law? Tomorrow you'll be famous all over Pedra Canga."

"What're you talking about, you spiteful wench?" bellowed Pulquéria. "Is it my fault a ghost appeared to me and not to you? Is it?"

"And since when is seeing a ghost some kind of privilege? Let's leave the souls at peace and have some respect for the inhabitants of the other world."

Neco Silvino tried to intervene by asking his wife to keep calm, but Maria Belarmina was possessed: "Keep calm my foot! I can't tolerate this lying busybody. Why don't you ask her what she was doing all by herself at that time of night on the Mangueiral estate? You can be sure it wasn't anything good. Serves her right. Her boyfriend didn't show up and sent the Wolfman in his place. Ha ha! That's a good one."

"Pull in your fangs. You're just jealous because you know men are attracted to me. Who'd look at a sack of potatoes like you?"

"Attracted to you? All they want is to get into your pants, that's all. No wonder they call you Miss Availability."

"Go to hell. I'm not staying here a minute longer. I don't know what I was thinking of to accept Neco's invitation."

Neco Silvino, disconsolate, didn't even try to convince Pulquéria to stay. He knew his sister very well. He knew no power on earth would make her change her mind. Pulquéria was a happy person, very even-tempered, but when she got angry–which rarely happened–don't go near her because she was dangerous. Fortunately, her wrath was short-lived. Pulquéria was incapable of holding a grudge against anyone. It was best to let it pass; later everything would sort itself out. Isn't that what always happened?

Bᴇɴᴛᴏ Sᴀɢʀᴀᴅᴏ was a man of few words. A widower for more than ten years, he lived alone, took care of the house, the garden, and a small chicken coop in back. Felícia helped from time to time with the housecleaning and had also done his washing since the days of his late wife Manoelina. The couple had never had children. They traveled a lot and, according to Felícia, had once even gone abroad.

"The house was a jewel. Dona Manoelina was very neat, well organized, and liked to see everything shiny and clean," Felícia said.

"What appealed to me more than anything about the two of them was that they were always hugging one another, like real lovebirds. It was a pleasure to see them together on Sunday walking to church," Maria Belarmina added.

"I don't know where you got that idea," said Neco Silvino. "As far as I know, Bento Sagrado isn't Catholic and doesn't follow any other religion. He does read lots of books, though. He's a wise man. That's why people come from all over to consult him about the law and other things. There's nothing you can ask the man that he doesn't know."

"All right. But one thing you can't deny: The two of them were crazy about each other."

"Of course I can't," Neco Silvino answered. "And who can? Their love was a beautiful thing to see. The proof of it is that Bento Sagrado never remarried. And not for lack of possibilities. They say that even now there are young women who still hope to catch him."

I'd never spoken with Bento Sagrado. I recognized him by sight and knew of his character through the opinion of the eldest residents of Pedra Canga. Only once, when I was in my teens, he came to my house to talk with my father. They spoke in a low voice on the porch, and I never learned the precise reason for the visit. I asked my father but he evaded the subject: "Business talk between men, daughter. Girls wouldn't understand such things."

I didn't give up. I asked mother why such secrets. She laughed and explained there wasn't any secret; Bento Sagrado had come to the house to buy Velvet, a horse, from my father.

"They've agreed on a price and tomorrow your father is going to Mr. Bento's house to deliver the horse to him."

"Isn't Daddy going to have a horse anymore?" I asked, hiding my sadness, for I was very fond of Velvet.

"Yes, he is. He's arranged to buy a horse from a man in Várzea Grande, and day after tomorrow he's going there to get the animal."

I looked for Daddy and asked him what he was going to name the new horse.

"Hummingbird," he said, smiling broadly.

"I don't like it. A hummingbird goes around sniffing every flower in sight without getting attached to any of them."

"What kind of talk is that, girl? I think you've been reading too many novels. Books like that just fill your head with fantasies."

I went to meet Bento Sagrado at twilight, at the door of his house, where I found him sitting in a rocking chair, reading a thick book whose title I couldn't make out. He interrupted his reading, cleared his throat, smiled, and said, "Ah, so we have the honor of a visit from our author. Let's go inside. Make yourself at home."

I accompanied him, somewhat ill at ease. As soon as I sat down in the living room I tried to explain immediately that I didn't consider myself a writer. I hadn't published anything yet and was just putting some ideas down on paper–

"But that's what matters. The act of creation. The search for forms that make possible continuous discoveries in your relationship with yourself and with the world," he interrupted, brusquely.

Bento Sagrado's powerful personality disarmed me from the start. As he spoke I could see he was measuring his words. Everything had meaning, his discourse came from within, nothing was gratuitous. His words possessed warmth and melody. But they gave off a savage energy that disturbed me immensely.

I almost forgot what had brought me there. Without knowing just where to begin, not wanting to appear nervous, I asked straight out what he thought of the story that people were telling about the Vergare house.

"That it changes colors according to its emotions? The people of Pedra Canga always looked upon that house as a symbol of hidden forces, arrogance, and evildoing, both because of the Vergares' past and because no one had access to the Mangueiral. Now that it has become available, they still attribute powers to it; they can't see it as an ordinary house in ruins."

I argued that many people had heard weeping and moaning in the ruins and that some had even seen shapes, while others had felt strange vibrations as they approached the site.

"The Vergares were very powerful. They mistreated many people for many years and were never punished by human justice. It's natural that when such power ceases to exist, the people see a divine punishment in everything, that they create myths and attribute to the supernatural any fact that, in different circumstances, would be nothing but a commonplace. It's a way of their feeling avenged, or compensated, if you prefer.

"Do you want an example?" he continued. "The standing walls, with neither doors nor windows, full of openings, form channels or funnels, located in different places. When the wind blows, it produces strong resonances that many have interpreted as moans, cries, screams."

"What about the shapes? Many people claim to have seen them roaming about the house."

"It could be. There have been lots of beggars wandering through the area lately. The ruins are a good place for them to spend the night."

"Then you think that everything people say about the Mangueural is just a story?"

"I didn't say that. I'm referring only to those absurd rumors."

"Then how would you describe the course of the Vergare family?"

"Solely in light of the facts. In my opinion, everything fits into a historical cycle. I witnessed the ascendance of the Vergares. They became rich through betrayal, robbery, bribery, and murder. Over the years they made enemies who swore vengeance. It's true that most of them are dead, but the younger generation carries on the struggle. Sooner or later what happened was bound to happen. The Vergares reaped what they sowed. One thing I can state without fear of contradiction: The Vergares' power was based solely on money. They were materialists. They never concerned themselves with the spiritual side."

In one last effort to counter Bento Sagrado's theories, I appealed to the name of Marcola: "Would you doubt Marcola's word?"

"Never."

"But her opinions are totally opposite yours on the subject...."

"We are made of different stuff. I'm a stubborn rock planted in the ground that doesn't dare to roll down ravines. Marcola is water, a flowing river that brings forth blossoms wherever it passes, turns into a waterfall, and finally enters the bowels of the earth."

With a tired expression, and sadness in his eyes, he had barely stopped talking when he rose and asked me to excuse him because it was time to go to sleep.

"Old people go to sleep early and get up before dawn. Ask your grandfather Zé Garbas. Good night, Miss Tereza."

"Good night, Mr. Bento."

"Please, St. Barbara, don't let it happen again. I promise to fast for three days if you hear my plea."

Maria Belarmina, rosary in hand, was trying to reach an agreement with the lady of storms. She was afraid. The sky darkened suddenly, the animals were restless, there was a leaden feel to the air– No doubt about it: Another awful tempest was on its way.

"Oh Lord, and that wretched old fool isn't home yet. You can be sure he's at the bar and doesn't even realize the world's about to end."

She was right. Neco Silvino didn't notice the weather outside, drinking with his friends, playing pool, chatting between games. When lightning began to streak the sky and the first thunderclaps broke, everyone tried to find his way home. Heavy rain wasn't long in coming. In uncontrolled fury the wind began to whine and howl, at first as if it were far away but soon the wind and rain took control of the air, deafening the people of Pedra Canga and maddening the livestock.

"It's one of the worst storms ever," said Maria Belarmina, drawing close to her husband, who had just come in. "Just like the night of Mr. V.'s death. Good Lord in heaven, what do they want this time?"

"They who?" asked Neco Silvino.

"I don't know. The spirits that wander about without rest. I'm not going to say their name 'cause I don't want to attract them here to the house."

Neco Silvino agreed with his wife. He remembered very well the experience of that earlier night. Everything was just the same. He felt helpless in the face of the threat of a new attack by the forces of the Mangueiral. If only Marcola were there... He called his wife and asked why she hadn't invited her friend.

"I sent Helmet Head specifically to her house to bring her here, but she wasn't home. He said he asked the whole neighborhood and nobody knew where she was."

"But how can that be? She didn't just disappear into the wind."

"Don't talk nonsense, Neco. My friend must be well sheltered at this very moment, maybe at Felícia's."

"I'm not all that worried about her, really. The woman has a guide inside her who'll never let her perish. I'm asking because I wish she was here with us, like last time..."

Felícia was at Vicência's house. She had gone there to handle the birthing of Carlita, the old matriarch's granddaughter. The large family was gathered that night for the birth, but the storm left them so bewildered that they forgot about the woman in labor. With a candle burning in the small chapel, they asked St. Barbara for protection.

Felícia also remembered that earlier night. The noises coming from the Mangueiral were the same, with the difference of a woman's cry that stood out above all the rest. Vicência, an octagenarian and well into her dotage, trembled in fear without the slightest notion of what was happening. Suddenly she yelled, "Isn't anyone going to help that poor woman? Her husband is beating her like she was a mongrel dog. It has to be Alzira, Salgado's wife. A woman with no self-respect. She takes a beating every day and still doesn't get rid of the animal."

"Grandma, how many times have I told you that Alzira died over five years ago?" Carlita answered, writhing in pain.

"Of course she didn't die. Just yesterday she was here asking to borrow a cup of rice. And you people say I'm the one who's senile. Young folks nowadays don't have the memory to keep track of what went on yesterday. At this rate, who's going to tell the history of the old folks?"

"Oh God, and now this," moaned Carlita.

The outside world became lost, dominated by strange beings fighting among themselves for possession of something hidden from the reality that could be seen with eyes. At times the noise seemed like bodies in a struggle in which were mixed speech in every tone, shouts, sobs, cries for help, and mocking laughter.

Again, darkness reigned over Pedra Canga. Again, the people delegated their fate to the saints.

"I place myself in God's hands. He knows what he does," said Ludovica, clutching the worn beads of her greasy rosary, evidence of her years of devotion and love for the Eternal Father.

At the Open Heaven, Genu gave the orders:

"Girls, nobody works tonight. Send the customers home and let's close the Heaven. I have to listen to my heart. The devil's on the loose and woe to whoever dares step outside. He'll get gobbled up without a trace."

My mother covered the mirrors in our house so as not to attract lightning and said that the storm was threatening to put an end to Pedra Canga. My father asked for calm, strung up the hammock, and went to sleep as she said, "The old folks always said you shouldn't sleep during a storm because your spirit floats in space and can get carried off by the wind. Then you never wake up."

But do you think Daddy paid the slightest attention to the warning? In a matter of minutes his snoring could be heard throughout the house.

Lúcia Palma, my friend since childhood, was at

Hortênsia Flores's house the night of the storm and said that she heard the seer repeat countless times an odd phrase of which she didn't understand "beans":

"The avengers have fulfilled their task. The time has come. The maiden in white will be buried when night falls."

The storm grew in intensity, rending the hearts of people to release the fear that disorients and dispels any thought of peace. When something exceeds the control of an entire community, panic sets in, "gets in the saddle and digs in its spurs," as my grandfather Zé Garbas would say. And that was just what happened. Pedra Canga had lost its foundation and was teetering crazily on life's seesaw. By all the deities, how much longer?

A terrible roar shook the entire area. The earth trembled. The howling came from deep below. It was felt through the feet. It was as if the earth were being torn asunder to cast a living monster into its entrails.

Then everything became hushed. Only the heavy rain continued until morning. Relieved, the people breathed deeply and fell into a sleep, exhausted from the battle. Against whom? Who could say?

It was a lovely day, one that promised sunshine. How good to look around and see that life had returned to normal. Many thought it had been a bad dream, one of those that you have when you overeat and go right to sleep.

Someone brought the news: The ruins of the house had disappeared.

"The earth swallowed them up," my grandfather said. "Nothing there but a huge hole."

"It was buried. The proof is that you can see a pile of dirt on top of it like a fresh grave," Smoking Snake said.

"The ground above it's smooth as can be. There's not a sign of the foundation," Pulquéria argued.

All of Pedra Canga went to see with their own eyes. They saw. No sign of it. And the place was even covered with grass... And a tarumã tree that hadn't been there before. Lemon trees and orange trees. But where in heaven's name had those plants come from?

"What a short memory people have!" said Felícia. "They're looking in the wrong place. Where the house used to be, nothing is growing. It's just an empty field. Nothing but tamped earth. A good place to build another house."

"A good place to build a church," Ludovica retorted.

"Church, my foot," said my grandfather Zé Garbas. "Isn't St. Gonçalo's enough, with Father Guilhermino as shepherd for Pedra Canga's sheep? What we need is a dance hall with a huge porch and lots of music, so people can dance till they drop." He did a pirouette in the air, trying to demonstrate that he still had a supple body.

Pedra Canga awoke to excitement. There were new people at the Mangueiral. Who? A band of gypsies. In the middle of the night they had set up their tents and by morning were occupied with their routine tasks–washing clothes, cooking, feeding the children–like any large family.

They acted as naturally as if they had been there a long time. They treated people like old friends, without formality. They spoke Portuguese, but when they didn't want others to understand their conversation they diverged into a complicated language that Christ himself couldn't have deciphered.

The girls were pretty, showy, in long braids and bright full skirts. They were mainly interested in approaching the boys.

"Want your fortune told? Past, present, and future? It's all written in the lines in your palm. Come closer, young man, don't be afraid. Hmm... I see that your life line is long and your fortune line shows you're going to be a very rich man. If you want to know more, cross the palm of my left hand with silver."

The tents were numerous, almost all of them the same size. At the largest a kind of Council, made up of old men, was meeting to consider important questions for the tribe. Sometimes they fell silent, their faces grave, puffing on long pipes. At other times they argued in loud voices; they would fight, then smooth things over and embrace one another like brothers, laughing uproariously.

"Have you noticed that the largest tent was erected exactly on the spot where the Vergare house stood? Don't you find that strange?" Pulquéria asked.

"One thing has nothing to do with the other," replied Maria Belarmina. "That's just a dirty, ragged tent that those down and out tramps set up on the ground. The Vergare house was like a palace."

"Dummy! You don't understand anything. I was talking about the coincidence of the tent occupying the same spot as the house, that's all."

"Well, to me that doesn't matter a bit," Maria Belarmina continued. "The Mangueiral is huge. They chose that area just like they could have chosen any other."

I couldn't help thinking about the radical change in the landscape. What had previously been a dark and forbidden world was now luminous, colorful, open. The freedom of the gypsies, in contrast with the enslavement of the African blacks who, on that very spot, had endured such horrors and even died at the hands of the masters of the Mangueiral.

The gypsies danced through the night. They sang, played the fiddle, the guitar, flutes and other instruments. They celebrated the freedom of their chosen way of life. Unceasing happiness was in their laughter, in song, in music.

In the slave quarters, black people fell ill and died of sadness. At best, they sang a melancholy song that recalled their lost freedom, but instead of bringing comfort it was a thorn pricking their hearts, lacerating their souls, edging their minds toward madness.

The residents of Pedra Canga never tired of watching the strangers, alternating between curiosity and fear. Some recalled tales told by the old folk in which gypsies–always untruthful and treacherous–even spirited away children.

"Is it true that you people steal children?" Pulquéria asked a husky gypsy with graying hair and an aquiline gaze.

"It's not true because we know how to make our own. Want to see for yourself? Let's go over behind that trash heap and I'll show you."

"See what it got you, you hussy? Why do you have to talk to people you don't know?" said Maria Belarmina.

"As if it mattered to me," Pulquéria answered. "I like them. They're a different kind of people. They sleep on the ground, cook in copper pots, sing, dance, fight, wear colorful clothes, and, best of all, they don't have any government. Nobody tells them what to do. They roam the world freely, without shackles or halters. They don't settle down anywhere. It's beautiful. How I envy them!"

"You're a born anarchist," said Maria Belarmina, shaking her head.

Two weeks after the gypsies' arrival, we heard that they were going to celebrate the wedding of Isabel, a young, dark, and pretty gypsy girl, and Juanito, an extraordinarily strong and handsome young man with whom several Pedra Canga girls had secretly fallen in love. A perfect couple whose images would adorn the romantic dreams of the area's young girls for a long time.

The day of the wedding arrived. From early morning the public, ever hungry for novelty, gathered around the encampment, pressing together, not wanting to miss the least detail. Nor did they, as the comments indicate:

"What a beautiful party. We've never seen anything like it around here," said Felícia. "I cried from emotion during the ceremony, though to tell the truth I didn't understand a word of what they were saying. But there was so much feeling... I couldn't resist. I cried like a calf that's lost its mother."

"The bride was lovely in her gown of white fustian

146

decorated with lace. And what about the wildflowers in her headdress? How romantic!" said Luíza Branquinha.

"And the groom. What a good-looking young man! Dark hair, dark eyes, a lovely smile, teeth white as snow. And very well dressed, all in white, with a red satin kerchief around his neck–he looked like a prince," sighed Pulquéria, the dreamer.

"And he danced with the bride all night long. They're so much in love... They were made for each other," Luíza Branquinha concluded.

"The banquet was a huge success. They had everything: roast suckling pig, turkey and stuffing, lamb, and kid goat. Barrels and barrels of wine and beer. Sweets of every kind. Such abundance!" said Celestial Archangel.

My grandfather Zé Garbas–who had become close friends with the gypsies, no one knew just how–was the only Pedra Canga resident to take part directly in the party. He ate and drank to his heart's content, as if he had enjoyed that friendship since childhood. He joined the musicians during the dance and coaxed the most incredible sounds out of his guitar in accompaniment to the gypsy melody that filled the air with vibrant chords.

The dance lasted through the night. Their joy touched me deeply. Such energy. They never once stopped dancing. Their bodies as light as feathers wafted on the wind, they formed a circle around the bridal couple.

"Beautiful, beautiful," Big Tomás repeated, enchanted.

I recalled the Vergares once more. What must it have been like in their time? The ballroom packed, the orchestra playing waltzes, the couples swirling about on the same floor now trod upon by gypsies? But what about happiness? Could they have been as joyful as these people? Could they dream and spread joy, cast off the bonds from their own bodies with no thought for the chains that imprisoned other bodies? Could they, even for a single instant, have imagined that the freedom of movement they sought in dance was infinitesimal compared to the fettered liberty of the slaves' lives?

The party went on late into the night. The movement of those in attendance diminished as the hours wore on. The next day, Monday, they had to get up early to work. I don't know who was the last to leave. I know that only one went home at daybreak–my grandfather Zé Garbas. He arrived merrily singing a gypsy tune that he'd learned from his new friends. He said it was a love song and that he would never stop singing it, just as he would never forget the marvelous night he'd spent in the company of gypsies.

"What a passionate people! Ah, if I were younger..."

"What would you do?"

"I don't know, granddaughter, but I think I'd take to the road with them. I'd get to know the world, see other countries, sleep in the open air, with the sky and the stars for cover. Free as a bird. What more does a man need?"

"Do you think you'd be happy like that?"

"Completely. I'd be in seventh heaven."

Early the next morning, Tuesday, there was an insistent knock at our door. My mother went to answer it.

"I'm coming, I'm coming. What's the rush? You'd think they were about to hang somebody's father."

From my room I recognized Aunt Sinhara's voice recounting something I couldn't make out. Mother began to cry and wail.

"By Our Lady, what are we going to do?"

I jumped out of bed in fright, ran to the living room, and asked what had happened.

"It was your grandfather."

"Is he sick?"

"No. If only he were."

"Then what was it?" I asked, expecting the worst.

"Your grandfather ran away during the night. He took his guitar and went off with the gypsies. The only thing he took was the clothes on his back and the sandals Emiliano made for him. Your grandmother is inconsolable, the poor thing. She can't stop crying. I wonder where he is right now."

"He's in seventh heaven," I answered, laughing, watching amazement spread over my mother's face.

I WANTED TO LOOK for Marcola the day after the storm, but the arrival of the gypsies, my grandfather's flight, and the illness of my dog Mascot had me so busy that I kept putting off the visit. One night I dreamed about a little girl saying she wanted to talk to me. Early the next morning I knocked at Marcola's door. Silence. I went around the house, looked for her in the back-yard, then knocked on her rear door. Nothing. Suddenly I felt uneasy when I remembered she hadn't been seen since the storm. Where was she? Maybe down by the river washing clothes?

"Good morning, missy, I was expecting you. I knew you'd come looking for me."

Marcola was smiling, wearing white as always, her skirt tucked around her knees and her feet in the water. She was washing a white hammock with blue embroidery that showed its long use. I asked about her health and told her I was worried because I hadn't seen her lately.

"Yes, but if I hadn't sent a message last night, you wouldn't have come today, would you?"

"I didn't get any message. I dreamed about a little girl–"

"And isn't that the same thing?" interrupted

Marcola. "When is missy going to get the courage to look directly at the reality she insists on calling a dream? Progress along the way of knowledge can be very slow if you're afraid to untie the rope to the canoe. You think you're going to get lost in the reaches of the river and forget that the oar is in your hands."

Finding no reply, I continued looking at Marcola, who returned to her task with the hammock. She rinsed it thoroughly, then asked for my help.

"Take off your sandals. Put your feet in the water and help me wring this hammock. It's too heavy for me. I'm not as strong as I once was."

I did what she asked, though I knew full well she could have done it by herself. Side by side with Marcola, the crystalline waters of the Coxipó lapping against my legs, I felt my body become light, and I departed from myself and went walking along the riverbank. I saw leaves dancing in a whirlwind and understood that colors have sound when the purple of the passion-flower gave forth a melody completely different from the yellow of the pumpkin blossom. The daisy's white is a soft waltz. The carnation's red, an ardent and sensual tango.

We finished wringing the hammock. Only then did I notice that Marcola had placed her right hand on my head and, with her left hand, sprinkled water on my body. The ceremony lasted only a few seconds.

"Are you baptizing me or saying goodbye to me?"

"You don't baptize without consent. Separation is the journey through open country that we take when the time comes."

We went back together to her house. We entered the yard and sat beneath the leafy crown of the mango tree, which welcomed us with its friendly shade, easing the heat of midday. We began to talk, and I asked where she had been the night of the storm. She said she hadn't left the house.

"I spent the night on alert, sitting under the ridgebeam of my hut, in the company of my guides."

I replied that I didn't understand, because Maria Belarmina had sent Helmet Head to look for her and he swore she wasn't at home. Was he lying?

"No, the boy did as he was told. I saw him here. But he didn't see me because my body was on another plane."

I asked if she knew the Vergare house had disappeared during the storm and that people were saying it had been buried.

"It's true. It was buried. It was a struggle that lasted all night, because the forces that ruled the house didn't want to leave it. They wanted to torment the people of Pedra Canga."

"You spoke of a struggle. Do you mean there was a greater force that won out in the end?"

"Manu, my master, who lives in the center of the Earth, and Unam, the lady of the wind, seconded by sheaves of luminous energy, sowed white carnation petals and chanted in a circle, seven times, around the appointed spot."

"So you think we're free of the Vergares forever?" I asked anxiously.

"The festival of liberation was witnessed by all of Pedra Canga. The Mangueiral house shone with such light, music, and joy. Maria dos Anjos was dazzling! She herself chose the design and material for her wedding dress and picked the wildflowers for the bridal wreath. How lovely young Maria looked. Long braids falling to her waist, all in white, in the arms of her bridegroom Antônio, dancing endlessly. He was very handsome too. Such sweetness in those dark eyes that could see only Maria... A blessed and happy couple, overflowing with love. It was truly a celebration. The dance lasted through the night. In the morning, Antônio and Maria caught the boat and sailed away in peace on the crystalline waters of the Xamaná."

Marcola fell silent. As on the other occasions, she was looking at something beyond that which I could see. She lightly touched my arm as if saying goodbye. Our encounter, I knew, had ended.

MASTERWORKS OF FICTION
Green Integer Books

Masterworks of Fiction is a program of Green Integer
to reprint important works of fiction from all centuries.
We make no claim to any superiority of these fictions over others in
either form or subject, but rather we contend
that these works are highly enjoyable to read and,
more importantly, have challenged the ideas and language
of the times in which they were published,
establishing themselves over the years
as among the outstanding works of their period.
By republishing both well known and lesser recognized titles
in this series we hope to continue our mission of bringing
our society into a slight tremolo of confusion and fright at least.

Books in this series

Books in the Green Integer Series

BOOKS IN PREPARATION

Islands and Other Essays Jean Grenier
Operratics Michel Leiris
The Doll and *The Doll at Play* Hans Bellmer
[with poetry by Paul Éluard]
American Notes Charles Dickens
Prefaces and Essays on Poetry
William Wordsworth
Confessions of an English Opium-Eater
Thomas De Quincey
The Renaissance Walter Pater
Venusburg Anthony Powell
Captain Nemo's Library Per Olav Enquist
Selected Poems and Journal Fragments Maurice Gilliam
Utah Toby Olson
The Pretext Rae Armantrout
Against Nature J. K. Huysmans
Satyricon Petronius [translation ascribed to Oscar Wilde]
The Cape of Good Hope Emmanuel Hocquard
Yi Yang Lian
Traveling through Brittany Gustave Flaubert
Delirum of Interpretations Fiona Templeton
Rosa Knut Hamsun
Zuntig Tom La Farge
Looking Backward: 2000–1887 Edward Bellemy
Civil Disobedience Henry David Thoreau
Fool's Triumph Ioana Ieronim
Victoria Knut Hamsun
The Sea Beneath My Window Ole Sarvig